To Andy & Ruth,
New friends and perhaps
soon to be neighbors.
With love & friendship.
Jack
May 2023

Joab

Jack N. Lawson

Foreword by Drew Bridges

RESOURCE *Publications* · Eugene, Oregon

JOAB

Resource Publications
An Imprint of Wipf and Stock Publishers
199 W. 8th Ave., Suite 3
Eugene, OR 97401

www.wipfandstock.com

PAPERBACK ISBN: 978-1-6667-6796-4
HARDCOVER ISBN: 978-1-6667-6797-1
EBOOK ISBN: 978-1-6667-6798-8

"This is the story of King David told by his nephew and army commander, Joab, three millennia after the fact. Events now look quite differently from those as told by the court journalist, whose records have come to us in the Bible. In his sixth novel, Jack Lawson makes us look again at David—with compassion and love, knowledge, wit and humor—yet with eyes wide open at a man as quintessentially human as ourselves."

—SHLOMO IZRE'EL, professor emeritus of Semitic linguistics, Tel-Aviv University

"King David's personal complexity—as lover, father, warrior, and king—make him one of literature's most compelling characters. But Jack Lawson not only narrates with imagination and humor; his life of scholarship in Semitic studies gives the tale historical authenticity. The result is a fresh and nuanced portrait and an engaging read."

—RICHARD PRUST, co-author of *Personal Identity in Moral and Legal Reasoning*

"A lively and imaginative novel, *Joab* presents the story of David in genre-bending ways that are sure to intrigue, surprise, and disrupt what readers thought they knew about the shepherd boy who became king."

—ELAINE A. HEATH, author of *Naked Faith*

JOAB

This book is dedicated to the one who inspired it:
Andrea Cimino

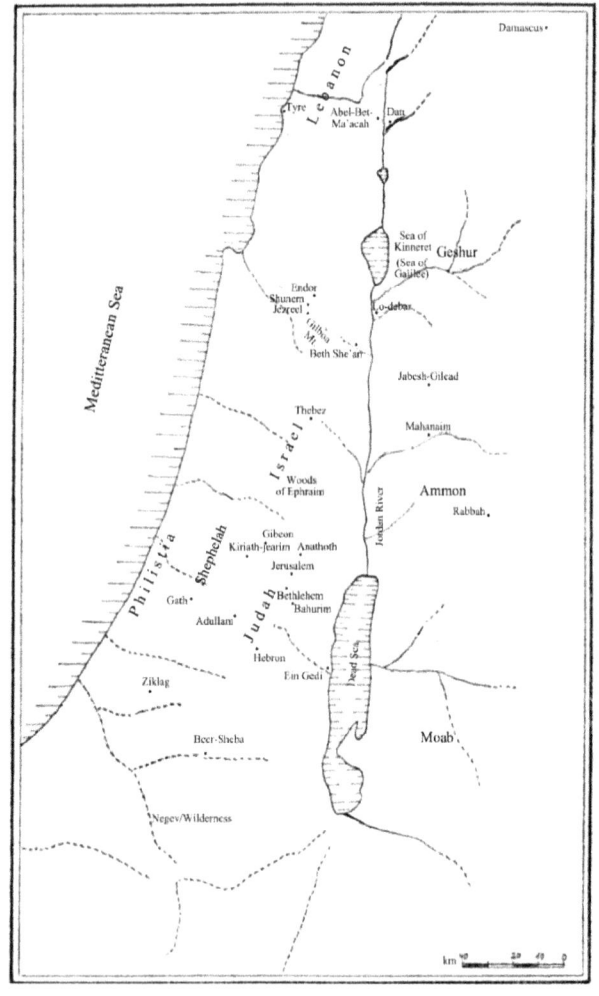

Israel at the time of Joab

Principal Characters

Abiathar — One of the two priests during David's reign

Abishai — Son of David's sister Zeruiah and brother of Joab

Abner — Commander of Saul's army; killed by Joab

Absalom — One of David's favorite sons; kills his half-brother, Amnon; rebels against David

Achish — Philistine king of Gath to whom David pledges loyalty when fleeing from Saul

Ahima'az — Son of Abiathar the priest

Ahitophel — An advisor to David who conspires against him

Amasa — David's kinsman; later commander of Absalom's rebel army

Amnon — One of David's sons; rapes his half-sister, Tamar; killed by Absalom

Bathsheba — Wife of Uriah the Hittite, a soldier in David's army. Raped by David.

Hushai the Archite — Friend and confidante of David

Ishba'al/Ishbosheth — Son of Saul who assumes the throne after Saul and Jonathan die in battle. His name is written alternately in the Bible

Joab — Son of David's sister Zeruiah and head of David's army

Principal Characters

Jonathan	Saul's son and successor; David's best friend
Mephibosheth/ Meriba'al	Lame son of Jonathan. His name is written alternately in the Bible. This is explained in the text. I have chosen to use Meriba'al.
Nathan	Prophet in David's court
Samuel	Prophet and last 'judge'/war leader of Israel
Saul	First king over Israel/Judah
Uriah the Hittite	High-ranking soldier in David's army, married to Bathsheba, murdered by David
Zadok	One of David's two priests
Ziba	Servant to Meriba'al, Jonathan's son

Foreword

I AM NOT A scholar of religion, but I grew up in the rural American south, so all my narratives for living are biblical. From David and Goliath to the prohibition against casting the first stone, such stories guide the way I think.

Jack Lawson is a scholar, thoughtful and pleasingly provocative. The following paragraphs suggest who should be rewarded by a reading of this book, and why.

Until the bookmobile started regular trips up our dirt driveway, the Christian Bible was one of few books in my childhood home. Our family Bible featured lovely colorful prints of many key events, from the nativity scene to the crucifixion of Jesus. A print of Absalom hanging from the tree by his hair, his chest punctured by the arrows, frightened me but intrigued me.

There were also a dozen or so prints of what Jesus might have looked like. I was always skeptical of the long-haired Charlton Heston version. Later I recall my pastor saying Jesus was a "rough looking Jew." At the time, I didn't quite translate this to an image, but slowly, certain puzzlements crept into my mind, such as foreskins presented as proof of victory in battle. I read Genesis 6 but never talked to anyone about it. It never came up at my church.

I started college at a small Christian junior college where religion courses were required. I had one professor who taught a course on "minor characters of the Bible." She was more than a little obsessed with Leah the tender eyed and with Matthias, the replacement for Judas as the twelfth apostle. I don't remember

much about what she wanted us to understand about the signifi-
cance of these characters, but I did come to realize that there was
much more to these "Bible stories" than the commonly shared
lessons.

It was in the above context that I read the story of Joab as
presented here by Jack Lawson. The narrative is written in a non-
traditional form. The reader will need a few pages to settle into the
reading of it, but it works. Joab is the narrator, welcoming to the
afterlife a "stranger" who seeks knowledge. Anticipating his guest's
questions, only Joab speaks as he takes the still living stranger on a
journey that tells the story of King David.

So, what does the stranger learn? I believe he learns the answer to the question of why this Hebrew literature has survived
and become the inspiration for all manner of artistic expression.
It is not—and please forgive me if I give offense—for anything one
would call biblical inerrancy, but because it is the story of the human condition. The stranger hears a story of love, hate, loyalty,
betrayal, cruelty, forgiveness, madness, lust, or any other desire,
longing, or loss one may name.

As I moved on through my education, biblical images were
never far away. As an English major I was captured by Steinbeck's
East of Eden. I graduated from medical school and moved on to a
forty-year practice of psychiatry. I marveled at why so many men-
tally disturbed people experienced variations of religious content
within their hallucinations and delusions. I remember one conversation with a patient who finally forgave herself for her anger;
she came to understand that anger is not a deadly sin because
even Jesus felt angry when he threw the money lenders out of the
temple.

So why read this book? I am not finished trying to understand myself, my world and culture. Jack Lawson's invitation to
hear a possible, perhaps probable, account of Joab's thinking about
his experiences is an opportunity for useful reflection. Anyone,
scholar or otherwise, who remains curious about one's cultural

origin story, this ancestral story, should find real intellectual and perhaps spiritual rewards by this reading.

Drew Bridges MD
Distinguished Life Fellow of the American
   Psychiatric Association
Author of *Family Lost and Found*, *Billion Dollar Bracket*,
   The Second-Greatest Baseball Game Ever Played,
   and *A New Haunt for Mr. Bierce*.

Introduction

IN THE BIBLICAL ACCOUNT of King David, Joab—David's nephew and commander of his army—is far too often either overlooked or simply a background figure taken for granted, yet he is absolutely essential to David's success. In today's parlance, Joab was David's 'Fixer;' he was the 'power behind the throne' or 'king-maker.' Reading about David's rise to power and his struggle to maintain that power, with the focus squarely on Joab, gives one a completely different appreciation of the David 'legend.' The author particularly wants to acknowledge the work of Meir Sternberg, which has added much to my interpretation and understanding of certain narratives surrounding King David. Thanks also to Shlomo Izre'el for his careful reading of the manuscript and useful comments. All direct and indirect speech has been translated from the Hebrew by me.

Despite reasonable scholarly opinions as to the order in which the chapters/events in Samuel should be read, I am following the narrative presented within the received text of the Hebrew Bible/Christian Old Testament. The author is fully aware of scholarly reasons for rearranging passages for the sake of continuity, but this has not impeded the telling of this ancient and compelling account. Wherever the Hebrew text is unclear as to its meaning, I have resorted to other early versions, particularly the Septuagint— the Greek translation of the Hebrew Bible in the 3rd century BCE.

As regards the names of the many characters and places, I have resisted the urge to transliterate them more in keeping with my knowledge of biblical Hebrew and have left them as found in most English versions of the books of Samuel. For those unfamiliar with 1 and 2 Samuel, it might behoove you to read through them before reading this novel.

Finally, at the end of most chapters, you will find bullet points for consideration or discussion.

One

Sheol, Paradise . . . or Thereabouts

WE ALL LIVE TWO lives—the one we are given, like yours, right now, and the life of memory—such as mine. But surely you must be aware of that as you are here, now, in this place that you consider the realm of the dead, but which we who live here know as life continuing. When I first arrived here, I would have been flattered that someone would have sought me, as few are those who come to this place—and return!

Why should you be surprised at my laughter? It is only the earth-bound living who carry the burdens of life, as you will come to see—if not now, then in the future. But come, you have sought me out for a reason, and of that, I am keen to learn. Is it for me, Joab, or perhaps of another that you have ventured here?

Ha! You blush! So very amusing. I was a man of war, and as such was consumed by military matters. I had little time for niceties such as embarrassment or emotions that were left to lovers, children or women. And when drained of their life blood, whether by sword or old age, the "dead," as you consider them, no longer blush. So, tell me, Stranger, why have you sought out Joab? Here I sit before you.

My relationship with David? Which David? King, my uncle, shepherd boy, upstart, murderer, rapist, adulterer, poet, "swinging little guitar man?" Which?

Oh, you are surprised by humor! Do you think that we who live in this realm know nothing of what passes on time-bound,

1

gravity-laden earth? Or that we have no traits of our humanity? Everyone you read about in your history books is here. You can use the same conjuror's trick to find them as you did me. Yes, kings, presidents, writers, politicians, lawyers, peasants, streetwalkers, drug-addicts, rock stars—such as the one to which I alluded, they are all here. "Hell," you ask? Haven't you already discovered it amongst the living? Please take no offense! I am enjoying your company and there is much you can tell me about life as you know and experience it. Ah, but you want to know why *everyone* is here, and not separated into "heaven and hell." It is a fair question, and I will answer it, but I feel it is best left until later. None of us really expected what this life continuing would hold for us. You will come to see why, for you will experience scores of years and see much in the few moments you are actually here.

Let me ask you something, Stranger: how do I appear to you? How does Joab look to your eyes? What? Really? Yes, of course; I appear to you as I was nearly three millennia ago—armor and a sword—a figure you would attribute to a warrior in the so-called Iron Age . . . yet sadly for us Hebrews, it was our enemies who were more adept at forging iron. We were newcomers to such arts and generally wielded weapons of bronze, which were no real match against iron. Ah, your perception of Joab is becoming visible to me as well. Look! Everything still fits! But, then it would, wouldn't it? You have designed me, shall we say, as you feel I should appear. Here, let me run you through with my sword. You flinched! This really is too funny! No, Stranger, don't depart—please. Are you injured? Is there a wound? Of course not. Stay, for rare are those who want to see Joab—but, David, the "great David, the beloved-one" whom I loyally served . . . ah, many are those who wish to see him. Are you aware that his Hebrew name means "beloved?" And the root of the same word means "uncle!" Funny, that, as he was my uncle. Ah, David, he is popular with those who are able to make the journey here and perhaps more popular now—in the imagination of the living—than he was when flesh and blood. And I shall tell you of him—but what is more, you shall see him for yourself, as he was.

Have you noticed, Stranger, that we are not actually speaking? No more can I speak your earthly tongue than could you speak mine. Fascinating, is it not? It is one of the many true joys of life continuing—no need for writing, speaking or translating—which was so tedious in earthly living. Remember what the Psalmist wrote: "You know my thoughts from afar?" All of us here participate in such knowledge and communication.

Come. Walk with me a for a while. It will help you to adjust—as much as you can—to these surroundings, which are so familiar to me and so terribly bizarre for you . . . but then, you have managed to make the transition from earth-bound life to life continuing, so surely you can't be completely surprised. No? That's good. Take my hand. No, it's not a trick—and see, my sword is back in its sheath. No, I'm not laughing at you—my laughter is at myself, for as poets have said it, "As you are, I once was." Truthfully, I am a little envious of your earth-life. I enjoyed being a good soldier, living hard and fighting harder—and the spoils were often worth the toil!

Now, does my hand feel warm and real to you, or perhaps insubstantial? Is it that of a mere specter? Warm? That is a good sign. It won't be long before we can leave this particular—shall we say, meeting place?—and go to find answers to your questions, for there is so much which is not told in those scriptures of yours. The biblical account of David was largely compiled by the court *mazkir*. Ah, you are puzzled by the Hebrew term. Let's see . . . how to translate it?—for such Hebrew words are laden with meaning. Everything depends, of course, upon context. This is something too often overlooked by the living. In the ancient world—much as today—kings and rulers had scribes who kept records or annals of their activities: wars, lawmaking, tribute received, etc. But the *mazkir* was so much more than a mere scribe. Please—offer me some terms which would describe such a person today. Personal private secretary? Sounds very British. Recorder? Hmm . . . has the sound of a machine. Personal assistant? Seems more fitting for one of the modern world's business magnates. Court historian? You say it is often used by biblical scholars . . . perhaps, but little did he know himself to be writing "history." Reporter? Chronicler? Stop, Stranger! There are too many of your English terms for the *mazkir*. The keeping of a personal journal is popular in your world, yes? Well, perhaps we can agree that the court *journalist* kept a journal of the king's words and actions. Shall we call him the "court journalist" and leave it at that? Good!

By the way, your modern Bibles are so much handier than our scrolls—not that I read them much. No, as I said, I was a soldier. I read orders from my king and gave orders, which others wrote for me. But now there are computers and the Internet!—you should just listen to some of the scribes and rabbis speak of these things! How they envy modern technology! Perhaps our communication here is something like your Wi-Fi? After all, who knows?—except for the Creator, who holds time within the divine hands.

Soon I shall take you to the hill country of the land you call Israel, where our people settled. Stupid really, as the most fertile land was below us—in the gentle slopes of the Shephelah—between the Judean hills and the coastal plain—as well as down in the Jordan valley. We held the high ground, which was sometimes useful in battle, but our enemies often possessed the gentle land that provided better pasturage and yielded more fruit. And the Philistines!—their cities were more sophisticated than ours, for they had access to the sea and the influences that came from across the water. But such were the choices made by those who came before us. Complaining couldn't change it. We are all bound, to some degree, to our times. One sees more clearly with a few thousand years of hindsight!

Tell me, can you float now? No, not in the water—do you see water here? In the air! You have not brought earth's gravity with you. Well, try it! Yes, you must let go of my hand. Not bad—very nice, in fact. Why the floating? Understand this: were you to travel, as you will, to the "past," with the same density and vibration of earth, you might well experience the misfortune of remaining there—something for which you are woefully ill-equipped. Is a warrior a scientist? No, I can't explain it all, any more than I can explain how you came to be here. It's *what is*—it's the bigger reality, if you will. No, in order to travel with me you must be . . . how shall I say it? All words are difficult to explain it . . . you must be, shall we use the Hebrew word, *ruakh*: your spirit self? In that way you may watch, attend, listen—but not impact—those lives which have already run their course. Be patient, you will see . . .

I think you are nearly ready to travel to your destination, which provides the answers to your questions about David—and myself, yes. As regards David, I am only your guide. He could tell you himself, but I think it's better to watch him in action—don't you? We'll dispense with his childhood. I assume it's the man that interests you. Good. Please take both of my hands.

〜&

I see you are frightened. It is only natural. We are passing through the realm of those recently passed from the earth—which is to say one or two centuries by your measurement. Horrid, you say? Yes, it can be, but it is also a place of cleansing, unburdening . . . some experience it as judgment. The Catholic Christians have called it Purgatory, which is as good a name as any. Dante did quite a good job in his poetic description. You'd like him, I think. One only wonders how you will be received should you try to describe all of this to others when you return. You'll probably be thought mad! But such is the price of your curiosity which brought you here. I know I would not have believed you in my day, but then I was never a very spiritual man. Will you have to pass through here when you leave the earth? A reasonable question and I surmise you would not have asked had you not wanted to know the truth. Yes. Everyone passes this way. Our prophets and priests used to warn us about such things . . . alas, death is a stern teacher. Oh, come now. Don't take on so! Oh—that area? Yes, it does resemble a desert dust storm within a hurricane. What a din, eh? You have a keen eye—I could have used you as an archer! I rather suspect that you will not spend time *over there*. Even I, who have taken many lives, did not spend time *there*. Who then? Ah, people like that vicious Jew-hater, Hitler, and his cronies; Stalin—and all those who play loosely with others' blood; people who turned their early mistakes into an art—and a way of life. Yes, mass-murderers, your terrorists of today's world, those who abused children—the list could go on. They'll still be there when you pass over . . . in earthly terms, they will be there for generations, such were their crimes. We'll soon be past. Stop looking! Just focus on me.

Two

The Cave of Adullam
Between Bethlehem and Gath

YOU LOOK WHITE AS a ghost, Stranger! Sorry, but I cannot resist. See yonder, David appears! You can't see him? Try this: curl both your hands like tubes and place one in front of the other like one of your telescopes and peer through them. Anything? Now twist your hands to adjust your vision. Ha! The living are so gullible! Why do you scowl at me like that? Do I disappoint you as a departed spirit? Better you should learn now—one less surprise for you when you pass over.

Listen, Stranger, when I was a fighting man, our humor was that of soldiers—the crude sort—and pranks! Ha! Once, before we fought a band of Moabites, one of our spearmen, Abiel, had one of our camp artisans repair his spear. Let me tell you that this spear was beloved by Abiel and had several bronze bands around the shaft. Before we met our enemies, Abiel was fond of brandishing his spear, striking it against his shield, as the bronze point and embellishments glinted in the sun. It is also the case that Abiel was one of the tricksters in our camp and was often cruel in his jokes toward our artisan who had a withered leg and could not join the fighting. So, this artisan, whose name I no longer remember—it was thousands of years ago—ha! Now you are smiling; that's good! So anyway, the artisan decided to remove one of the bands, saw through the shaft and then replace the band—tightly, so as to hold the two halves together. Well, came the fight and there was Abiel, boasting to the Moabites how many of them he was going to slay. He lifted his spear, bashed it against his shield—and it broke in half! This I tell you in truth—for we here cannot lie to you—there was no fighting that day. Not only were my soldiers bent double with laughter—but so were the Moabites. They even bade us "shalom" as they left the field. Is it not amazing how laughter can make friends of enemies? Would that it were always so simple!

Now you seem more relaxed, Stranger. I am pleased for you. Death and the dead are only fearful for those who have seen so little of either. Now turn and look—there's your David. No, you cannot speak to him or he to you—everything here has already transpired. Consider how light, once emitted from its source, continues its journey through space. We are, as it were, simply catching up with the photons from actions done long ago. I thought it might be better to let David's actions, words and deeds speak for themselves. Then you can come to your own conclusions—what is the modern saying?—between "the man and the myth." I sense you prefer I stop talking.

So, Stranger, how does your David appear to you? Of course, he looks rough and unkempt—as do all of them. With David are his family, as well as a group of malcontents. They make quite a rabble to keep company with God's anointed, don't they?! See, there am I! The one with the scraggy beard and eager eye, nervously handling my sword. Ah . . . if I had only known what lay before me—but enough. It's done.

As your version of our scrolls teaches you, David, as you see him here, is on the run from Saul. He must change his hiding place at a moment's notice. Thus, there is not time for the luxury of bathing. Tell me, do you not find a bitter irony in the fact that we have two men anointed by the Almighty, with one seeking to destroy the other? I love your modern phrase, "spoiler alert!" Yes, even in the realm of life continuing there remain mysteries.

Don't mistake me, Stranger, but one almost has to pity Saul! He never asked for kingship over Israel—rather it found him in the person of Samuel—the same prophet who also anointed David. I cannot say I ever fully understood this anointing business. Take Saul, for example. The poor sod goes looking for his lost donkeys. He goes to Samuel for help—a man noted for having visions such as you are experiencing now—and ends up getting anointed as the first king of Israel! His confirmation that this was the Lord's intention was the fact that he would have three encounters after leaving Samuel. In the first encounter, Saul and his manservant would meet two men who would tell them that the animals they are seeking have been found; next they will meet three men carrying goats, bread and wine, and they will be offered loaves of bread; finally—and most interestingly—they will meet a band of prophets, whereupon the spirit of the Lord will fall upon Saul, such that he will become "another man," and prophesy along with the prophets. And this, Stranger, is where I feel all starts to go wrong for Saul.

Samuel tells Saul that once these events have transpired, he is to wait seven days for him, this man who was both prophet and priest for the Lord. But after seven days, Samuel had not appeared to instruct Saul as to what he should do—and his army is deserting him in the face of the Philistines. So, poor Saul offered sacrifices to seek the Lord's pleasure and direction. This, as you know, brings the wrath of Samuel, who tells Saul that the Lord has now rejected him as king. The poor fellow had barely commenced his reign when it was all over for him. It was only left for him to live out his tragic life and death. What? Wasn't there another case against Saul? Yes, you are correct in saying so, for surely it is in the first scroll of Samuel. When our scribes had two similar stories of how something came to be, they kept both. For, unless one were there to witness exactly what happened, the scribes felt it safer to keep both accounts, rather than remove one from the record. So, Saul was commanded to fight the Amalekites—Israel's mortal enemy since the days of the Exodus, when they sought to stop Israel's journey to the promised land. The Lord spoke to Moses and told him the remembrance of

Amalek would be erased from all memory and Israel would always be at war with Amalek. Saul was commanded not only to eradicate these people, but also all of their possessions, flocks and herds. But alas, the record shows that Saul and his army spared Agag, king of the Amalekites, as well as the choicest of their animals for sacrifice to the Lord. And for this transgression, the Lord rejected Saul as his anointed king over Israel. But who knows whether there were two such transgressions or only one? For Saul, the outcome was the same. Stranger—does it not seem to you in earthly life that there are those whose lives are seemingly determined while others apparently have free will? It is a common topic amongst those of us who live here. We shall revisit this question again.

In any case, for the rest of his life, whenever the Lord sent a spirit upon Saul, it was usually to torment him and to turn him into a jealous, homicidal maniac! So much for the Lord seeking "a man after his own heart!" Oh, rest assured the Lord hears every word I say . . . or think! Yes, of course, I believe in the Lord. Only a fool would not. But this I have learned: it is more important that the Lord believes in me—or I would cease to exist! Let me continue.

Anyone who has read the scriptures knows this is where David comes in. The Lord sends Samuel to the house of Jesse, whereupon he anoints David as king. In this soldier's opinion, the kingship of Israel never had a firm footing. After all, it virtually began with a civil war, and with David taking refuge for himself and his family in the towns and villages of our enemies. Had it not been for the likes of me, Joab, David's reign would have ended as quickly as that of Saul. Yes! I see the glint of recognition in your eyes. I sense you have read the scriptures closely. It really is all there for those with the eyes to see and who can discern between the overlay of human interpretation and legend. No, I am neither bitter nor jealous as regards David. Did I have my differences with my uncle when I walked the earth?—of course. I saw many of my men die for David's vanity—but of that, you will see for yourself.

First, see what destruction followed in David's wake. It all began in Nob, where David fled from Saul and begged the Bread of the Presence from the priest Ahimelech for himself and his fellows. He also received the sword of the Philistine, Goliath, for David has fled with no weapon. And now see—Saul has just learned of Ahimelech's helping David, through the mouth of Doeg the Edomite, a servant of Saul. See how Ahimelech and all his father's house and family are being summoned before Saul. Now we follow them to their unfortunate fate. No, Stranger, we cannot simply move ahead. If you truly wish to know David, then you must see with your own eyes what so many of us had to see. There! They stand before Saul, who is enraged. He wishes Ahimelech, his family, and all of the other priests dead. But see—the Israelites will not slay the priests of the Lord; yet sadly, neither will they stay the hand of Doeg, who not only slaughters eighty-five of the priestly caste—he also goes on to lay waste to the entire city of Nob—both its human inhabitants and animals. Such wanton waste and destruction! It is well you avert your eyes! In your time, men kill one another from afar, but we had no such luxury in our day upon the earth. Such slaughter was a close and messy business. These hands of mine have also worn the blood of many men.

Now let us see how David receives the news of Nob's devastation from its one survivor, Abiathar. Does David fly into a fit of rage and seek the death of Doeg? You already know the answer. David instead goes to relieve the town of Keilah from Philistine siege. Yes, I know, the scriptures say it was the Lord's will, but only David could attest to that. What I know is—in order to sate David's hunger, scores of innocent people had to die.

Come, Stranger, lest you think I am merely trying to discredit the name of my uncle, I will show you David's sense of honor—although his followers certainly felt differently. For this we move to Ein Gedi, not far from the Dead Sea—see how its lushness contrasts with the surrounding dry wilderness. Such is the value of a spring. What you are about to witness is one of scripture's amusing accounts, for it is the only time we read of a king . . . how shall I say it—taking a dump! And of all places, Saul goes into the very cave where David and some of his comrades are hiding. Very discreet of Saul to shit in private, don't you think, when most of his soldiers simply squat by the wayside? But I suppose that is the prerogative of kings, eh? Now listen! Hear how David's men urge him to have his day of vengeance on the man who seeks his life. They see it as a God-given opportunity. Well—who wouldn't? I was hiding elsewhere from Saul's army, but rest assured I would have been among those who wanted my uncle to finish Saul. I think it would have been a blessing to his poor, tortured soul. But your David is a man of contradictions. He still gives honor to the fact that Saul is God's anointed and refuses to end this conflict by killing him. Yes, Stranger, you are right; it does seem that the oil of anointing comes from a poisoned chalice. It is a bizarre situation in which the two messiahs are found. Watch as David slips from his hiding place to cut off a piece of Saul's cloak. Have you ever wondered what might have transpired had Saul detected David's presence? I can only believe there would have been bloodshed. You as well? Perhaps my uncle even wanted to precipitate such a crisis, in order to kill Saul in defense of his own life? Yes, I have asked him—not when we walked the earth—but following my "cleansing" period after passing from earthly life. You see, after arrival in life continuing, there is a still a period during which one still cares about the life one has left behind—why one decision was made as opposed to another, why one followed an order for no good reason. There is ample time to review one's life—for good or ill. Stranger, there is no avoiding it; thus, there is no use dreading it. I have come to know humanity fairly well in my centuries here, and judging from what I have seen, heard, and felt from your presence, you have nothing to fear when your life is reviewed.

Look! See how David slips from his hiding place and takes hold of Saul's cloak. As Saul emits his bodily noises while evacuating his bowels, David slices off a piece of the royal cloak. How could Saul remain unaware, you ask? Perhaps he had wax in his ears? I jest, for I have no idea. Or perhaps he sensed David's presence—as well as heard him—and simply waited for the death blow. Even in life continuing, we don't find all of the answers we would have liked on earth. In any case, we see Saul leaving the cave—perhaps relieved in more ways than one!—to rejoin his men and their hunt for David. Now watch as they are ready to ride away—David makes his appearance. He calls out to Saul as his lord and his king. Is this not amazing, as it is Saul who desires David dead? See how David shows to Saul the fringe of his cloak. He makes clear to Saul that, although he had every opportunity to kill him, yet he spared the life of the Lord's anointed. He even calls Saul "father."

Make no mistake, Stranger, David is now an easy target for Saul's men. He has given away his hiding place, so now both he and his men would be easy prey for the vengeful Saul. Hear now! David has finished speaking his case before Saul and the Lord. Attend well to Saul's words. "Is this your voice, David, my son?" Mark Saul well. Despite whatever sickness of mind plagues him, David's voice has pierced his heart and he is now overwhelmed by the indignity of his actions. It is as though the Lord has allowed Saul clarity of vision and thought for this brief moment. He acknowledges David's loving-kindness toward him, despite Saul's bloodlust with respect to David. Before his own soldiers, Saul admits that David has not deserved the contempt that he, Saul, has shown him, whereas David has only behaved in a righteous manner regarding Saul. Would that this irrational feud had ended there, Stranger, but as you well know, Saul's demented mind steers him back to his vendetta against David. Why, you ask? To answer that, you would have to know the very mind of God. I like the saying that many thinkers have used: "Whom the gods would destroy, they first make mad." It certainly seemed to be the case with Saul. Such a cruel fate for one anointed by God. When I walked the earth, there were many in surrounding cultures who considered being "touched by a god" the source of human madness. So too, it would seem, with our Hebraic understanding of anointing . . . but you can decide for yourself.

For consideration:

- Have you ever thought about how the geography/topography of Israel affected its development?
- Why would God have allowed two "anointed ones," leaving them to fight it out?

- Had you ever considered the importance of Joab in the story of David? Keep this in mind as you read this book.

Three

Gath and Ziklag, in Philistia

STRANGER, YOU KNOW THE account of David and Saul well enough to know that there continued the to-and-fro activity between them, driven by Saul's ever-changing state of mind. Yes, today you call it bipolar disorder and that seems a fitting description. With Saul, it worked like the lighting and extinguishing of a lamp. In one moment, he could clearly see his words and actions, but in an instant, he could lose all sense or reason. Why did people continue to follow him? Really!—need you ask? Only consider your own times. People fall into line behind the most self-centered, ruthless, and unscrupulous persons. Oh, either these humans want a "quiet life" or they hope to gain somehow from the person who leads them. Either way, most are usually disappointed—except those who are too stupid to see the results of their choices. In Saul's case, he had the added burden of having been anointed by God through Samuel. I'm sure there were the odd few who continued to put their trust in his having been anointed as God's chosen leader, but we have already witnessed what transpired when the Almighty withdrew his favor from Saul and anointed David—the very reason we are witnessing all of this chaos and violence.

But see, we have changed locations, for David is about to transfer his allegiance to Achish, the king of Gath, which is a Philistine city. Listen, for he is reasoning to his men. He feels resigned to dying by Saul's hand if he stays in Israel, so he convinces his family and other followers they have nothing to lose by pitching their tents with the life-long enemies of the Hebrew people, the Philistines. Rather ironic, don't you think, for God's anointed to desert God's chosen people for the Philistines? Ah—that hadn't escaped your notice either? There is a further irony in all of this—can you think of it? Good! Yes, Gath is the very town from which Goliath came! You are right—one couldn't make this up! So why all the fuss over David amongst both Jews and Christians? I mean, trying to trace the lineage of Jesus back to the house of David! And anyway, even if Joseph actually were from the family line of David—he wasn't the father of Jesus, was he? I'm glad you can laugh. It's taking all of the legends that have crept into one's faith too seriously which helps keep humans at war with each other and far from the actual love of the Creator, which those in life continuing now know.

Notice how David requests refuge in one of the outlying villages of Gath. I mean, after all, if six hundred armed men from your sworn enemies came to you for refuge, would you want them encamped nearby? And what a rough bunch they are now—they, and their women and children. Note the hesitancy as well amongst Achish and his advisors. From whence did the bounty or dowry for Saul's daughter Michal come—except from the two hundred Philistine men who lost their foreskins—not to mention their lives! Saul had only asked for one hundred! Well should it sicken you—but look throughout human history and you will find the same gross need for proof of slain enemies—be it scalps, ears, hands or foreskins. Wild animals kill without need for such macabre practices.

In any event, David's band of ruffians, among whom I was numbered, could either present a threat to Achish and the inhabitants of Gath or be a political coup—having this arch-Hebrew enemy and his fighting men changing alliances. So, David and his tribe are sent to Ziklag, some distance southeast of Gath. And from Ziklag, we Hebrew warriors rained terror on the local people: Amalekites, Geshurites and the Girzites—all tribes living in the

Negev, on the southern boundary of Israel. Let us watch David in action. I promise this is the only one of his raids I will show you.

Why did we slay not only the fighting men, but the women, the children, and the elders? It was David's order. Normally, the women would be sold or taken into concubinage, sometimes taking their children with them; other times children would be killed along with the aged, as they are simply more mouths to feed. Remember, Stranger, we had no refrigeration or canning procedures in our time. Unnecessary mouths were as large a burden as a drought. Yes, I understand, your question still obtains: Why did David have them all slaughtered? Perhaps to hide the fact that he was not conducting raids against his fellow Israelites? Perhaps in order not to enrich Achish with slaves? Truthfully, I know not. We were allowed to take their animals and other possessions as booty—but such would be the policy of almost any warlord. Loyalty is nearly always paid for in some manner—especially in such circumstances. But as you witness David here, his actions are those of a brigand—the sort who would have been hunted down by any civilized kingdom, then or now, for destabilizing the peace of the kingdom. In any case, David's raids against southern tribes work—but only for a time—for the day comes when Achish calls upon David and his men to go to battle against Israel. Not only that, but Achish also announces that David's brigade shall become his personal bodyguard—for life. Now there is no greater test for David's true loyalty.

For consideration:

- Had you ever reckoned with David's life as a brigand?
- Commentators have tried to defend David's allying himself with the Philistines as a ruse. Can you find proof for this?

Four

The Jezreel Valley

SEE YONDER: THE PHILISTINES are encamped at Shunem and, as far as Saul is aware, David is among them, while the Hebrews have made their camp by Mount Gilboa. None in David's camp actually knew what was going on in his mind. For all we knew, we were indeed going to fight against our fellow Hebrews—and why not? Saul and his soldiers had been hunting us like wild animals and wouldn't have thought twice about killing us if he had so ordered. Did Saul know that we were among the Philistine host? After sixteen months, word must certainly have got out. To be sure, there was talk amongst our men about why David hadn't killed Saul when he had the chance. At least it would have prevented this open warfare against our own people. But now, as for soldiers in any war, it was a case of kill or be killed—and most of us didn't fancy the idea of being dead. Note the flickering campfires . . . it would all be so beautiful were it not portending the deaths of so many which were to follow.

Look there: Saul is secretly leaving his encampment with two bodyguards. Once again you are right. He is on his way to consult the medium at Endor—to the north of the Philistine camp. Saul has found that the God of Israel will no longer speak to him, either by night, in his dreams, or by day, through prophets—or even by means of the Urim or Tummim, the Hebrew means of divining a "yes or no" answer by a sort of casting of lots. For once, Saul is in total desperation in the face of his enemies. Samuel is dead and none of the traditional means of hearing from the Lord are working for Saul—so why not try necromancy to contact the spirit of the departed Samuel? One could honestly say he didn't have anything else to lose.

Of course, the irony in this situation is that it was Saul who had driven out mediums and diviners, as their practices were contrary to the radical faith demanded by the Lord. Therefore, Saul has disguised himself, with the hope of not being recognized. Let us listen.

See how the woman fears entrapment, thinking this is a snare to catch her out. But Saul adjures her by the name of the Lord that no harm should befall her for consulting the dead. She asks upon whose name should she call, and when Saul responds with "Samuel," mark well how she reacts: with terror. What is that, you ask? If she is a medium, why didn't she know it was Saul who was approaching her? Ha! I see your humor is coming alive here in the "realm of the dead"—that was very good! In seriousness, I suppose one would have to admit that her skills are with the dead and not the living. Nevertheless, she now knows it is Saul who has come for her assistance, and thus is frightened for her life. Yet again, Saul reassures the medium and asks whom she sees. Now, Stranger, here I must explain. We Hebrews used the word *elohim* in a variety of ways. Yes, it can mean "a god" or "*the* God" or "heavenly beings" and more. But what the medium of Endor witnesses is the *elohim* which is Samuel, rising up before her. Inasmuch as you have come to life continuing, you will not be surprised to learn that what she saw was a figure not unlike my own. Perhaps I should coin the term "eternal being?" But mark well that Samuel is none too happy to be brought from the realm of life continuing. Mind you, I have never been called back to the world, but as I understand it, it is quite a shock to one's being. Here, as you are now experiencing it, we live like light itself. In an instant, we have been transported nearly three thousand years to see things that have already transpired— we think it and we are there! Poor Samuel has barely begun his life transition in this realm when he is called back by the medium. I expect you will experience something of that transition when you return to your life in the world. In any case, Samuel liberally shares his anger with Saul, who begs instructions from Samuel as to what he should do in the face of the Philistines. Listen! Samuel tells the forlorn king there is nothing more he can tell him that hasn't been said when Samuel still walked the earth. The Lord has abandoned Saul and there's the end of it. Could any man be more isolated or lonelier than Saul at this moment? Would that only the fate of Saul were at stake—but many more lives will be lost in the coming battle, and mourning will be heard throughout all Israel. Saul now collapses, as much from hunger as from despair, for he has not eaten for twenty-four hours—not a good idea when one is about to go into battle. Although Saul refuses even a morsel of bread, his companions—and the medium herself—convince him that he must take nourishment. The woman even kills her fatted calf and prepares it for Saul, and he finally eats.

For consideration:

- Saul's encounter with the medium at Endor is one of several examples of divination in the Bible. Note that her skill at calling up the dead Samuel is *not* ineffective—it has simply been forbidden for worshippers of Yahweh.

Five

Ziklag

NOW LET US RETURN in time—one of the advantages of life continuing—to David in the Philistine encampment, but before they set off to do battle with the Hebrews near Gilboa. Here we see them still in Aphek, engaged in what seems to be some sort of military parade. Look there! When the commanders of the Philistine army note the presence of David and his men with Achish, they rigorously object to his presence with their troops. They do not feel that David could be trusted to remain on their side once battle was joined and insist that Achish send David's contingent back to its lodgings at Ziklag when the Philistines go to meet the Hebrew army. Is it not fascinating that this Philistine king uses the Hebrew oath "as the Lord lives," when he speaks to David? "As the Lord lives, you have been honest and straightforward with me in all of our dealings." It is well you should ask, Stranger, was David truly a turncoat? All I can tell you is: to this point beyond time, I still do not know what David would have commanded us to do had we gone into battle amongst the Philistine host. Because of Saul's desire to see us eradicated, I know we would have fought our people, had David so commanded. But David has kept his counsel all these centuries long. Many have been those who impute only honorable intentions to David during our sojourn amongst the Philistines . . . why have I ceased speaking? Alas, I have found that being God's anointed does not necessarily change a man's heart or his choices.

He nevertheless remains mortal—and yes, I refer to David, who remains something of a conundrum to me.

Still, let us follow David and his men to Ziklag, which has been attacked by the Amalekites and burnt—but happily, the women and children have been spared, but taken as slaves, unlike David's raids on southern tribes. Having meted out terror and destruction to others, now David—and indeed all of us—become the recipients. He weeps along with all the others at the loss of their wives and young children. Now he must decide whether or not to pursue the Amalekites. As we have witnessed before, David consults the Lord with one of the few methods of divination sanctioned by our faith: the Urim and Tummim. Such was our only means of seeking the Lord's will when there was no time for dreams or no prophet at hand. The message he receives tells him to go after the Amalekites, and that he shall rescue all of the captives. What? That is a very good question, Stranger, and now you have given me pause. You are right that David asked two questions of the Lord, so did he cast the Urim and Tummim twice? Did he try the best out of three? Ha! You do amuse me, Stranger! I sense something of the cynic in you. Could David—or anyone—simply receive the answer he wanted? Oh, Stranger, I wonder whether you have spent too much time with me! But, as I have told you, in those days I was a man of war, a soldier. I know nothing of the priest's profession or the diviner's arts—nor that of the anointed's relationship with the Almighty. I followed the orders I was given. And, I must admit, at that point in my life, I was in awe of my uncle David.

See there—David and his six hundred fighting men set off in pursuit of the Amalekites. In this case, all are eager to restore their families and possessions. But their journey is hard, and after some time, one third of his men and animals are exhausted, so David allows them to remain by the brook Besor. The rest of our band followed the Amalekites, and with the help of an Egyptian slave abandoned by the Amalekites, we succeeded in overtaking our much-reviled enemy. In our fury we killed them all—except for those who had animals on which they could escape. All of our families were restored, along with our possessions. Perhaps there is no need to state that we took all of the Amalekites' belongings—such was, and still is, the nature of tribal war . . . and, in fact, it was our "pay." For the most part, none of us had other means of making money to support ourselves and our families at that time. But note what happens when our band reaches those who were too exhausted to continue our hunt of the Amalekites. Some among us felt that those who had remained behind should have no share in the spoils, as they had not participated in the fighting. See how little humanity has changed over the millennia? Here, David shows his uncanny knack for leadership in times of crisis. He states that it was the Lord who put our enemies into our hands and therefore all shall share equally in the spoils—even making it a legal statute from that time forward. Ah, your question is well put, Stranger. Let me answer you this way. Can you think of any leader or monarch in history who has not had to purchase his enemies' loyalty while at the same time rewarding his friends? No, I am not stating which is the case with David—you can decide for yourself as you watch him in subsequent situations. But do make note that David sends portions of the spoil to the elders of Judah.

For consideration:

- What do you think played a greater role in keeping David's men loyal to him?—his status as the Lord's anointed or his ability to deliver victories and loot . . . or perhaps fear of David?

Six

Mount Gilboa

LET US RETURN TO the north and the valley of Jezreel, which is overlooked by Mount Gilboa. What you are going to observe will not be sweet to your eyes. See, the battle is already joined and the Hebrews are suffering badly at the hands of the Philistines. No man should have to see his offspring die before him, but Saul's fate is to see Jonathan and his other sons brutally slain nearby him. The lineage of Saul is now utterly wiped out. There is no pretender to the throne, which is now David's. Yes, Stranger, war is simply organized butchery. The Philistine archers have identified Saul and he falls, wounded. Does he not make a pitiful character? It is even hard for me to watch him beg his armor-bearer to finish him, so that he cannot be taken alive, only to be taunted and tortured to death. But as you have read in the scriptures, his armor-bearer refuses to dispatch the Lord's anointed—even when the Lord no longer favors Saul. Thus, Saul's last act is to fall on his sword—the last but one act in his tragic life. I think there is no need to watch the death throes of Israel's army—they who under Saul had become the bane of the Philistines. The final act in the tragedy of Saul is the bestial way both his and his sons' bodies are hung on display from the walls of Beit She'an, only a short distance from here. Of all the creatures that have walked the earth, only humanity has gloated in such trophies of war. Saul's armor is collected and sent throughout Philistia, as proof of the glorious news that

Saul is dead. Perhaps the one saving grace for Saul and his sons is that their bodies are spirited away during the night by some brave survivors of the Philistine onslaught.

Ziklag

We return to the ruins of Ziklag with David and his warriors, after their slaughter of the Amalekites. A survivor—or perhaps simply a witness—of Saul's defeat comes staggering into view, his clothes rent and with dirt upon his head—these signs alone should have been a clear message to David, but perhaps he hopes for better news, despite all appearances. Hear how he asks for news of the battle. The news David receives confirms the condition of the man standing before him. Israel has been routed by the Philistine army and Saul and his sons are dead. Mark well that David seems suspicious of the man and his testimony, so he queries how he came to know that Saul was dead. He states that he was on Mount Gilboa by happenstance—although one wonders at how someone stumbles into a full, pitched battle! He says Saul asked him who he was, and the man replied, "I am an Amalekite." This admission, Stranger, probably sealed his fate, for the Amalekites have been the sworn enemies of the Hebrews since the time of the Exodus. He relates that Saul, gravely wounded, asked him to kill him, which he reports he did. And he has brought Saul's crown and armlet to David . . . perhaps he thought he would be rewarded for preventing the capture of Saul and for returning the emblems of Israelite kingship? In any case, he has certainly signed and sealed his death warrant, for David puts to him, "How is it you weren't afraid to put forth your hand to slaughter the Lord's anointed?" The hapless fellow! Even as a Hebrew, I have to ask how an Amalekite was to know who was or wasn't the anointed of our God? They had their own gods! But having just come from slaughtering Amalekites, it seems David's bloodlust for them has not settled, so he commands that the messenger be killed. Yes, Stranger, it is a wonder that all wells and springs do not run red with blood when one considers all the killing that has taken place on the earth.

Listen! Much as David had sung to comfort Saul when he was in one of his depressive moods, David now sings to express his grief and to comfort himself.

The beauty of Israel has been slain upon your high places;
How the mighty ones have fallen in the midst of battle!
Do not report it in Gath; nor in the streets of Ashkelon,
Lest the daughters of the Philistines rejoice,
lest the daughters of the uncircumcised exult.
O mountains of Gilboa, let neither dew nor rain be upon you,
nor the fields of offerings.
For there the shield of the mighty ones was defiled,
the shield of Saul, unanointed with oil.
From the blood of the slain, from the sword of the mighty ones,
Jonathan's bow did not turn away.
Nor did Saul's sword return empty.
Saul and Jonathan, beloved and delightful.
In life and in death, they were not separated.
They were swifter than eagles and stronger than lions.
O daughters of Jerusalem, weep for Saul,
Who clothed you luxuriously in scarlet,
Who adorned your clothing with ornaments of gold.
How the mighty ones have fallen in the midst of battle!
Jonathan, upon your high places, slain!
I am distressed on your account, my brother—Jonathan!
You were delightful to me Jonathan.
Such was your love to me that it surpassed the love of women!
How the mighty ones have fallen, and the weapons of war smashed!

My uncle did have a way with words, did he not? And, yes, with music as well. You are right. He bears something in common with that great composer, Mozart. You are perplexed? It's all in their names. Wolfgang Amadeus Mozart. Amadeus can be translated "beloved by God," and the root meaning of David is "beloved"—as well as "uncle." Is that not amusing, Stranger, as David is my beloved uncle? Yes, as always, so much is lost in translation, for languages bear entire cultures and ways of thought, and these simply vanish when translated. It amazes me how so many people on the earth become greatly exercised over the "literal" meaning of scriptures—to the point of wanting to kill those who disagree!

Stranger, *there can be no "literal meaning!"* All literal means is "according to the letter!" But what do letters mean unless they are formed into words? And, alas, words are only approximations of what we think and feel inside, and struggle to express. And there is always so much that is left unsaid—or unwritten, as you are beginning to see with the accounts of David.

For consideration:

- One would hardly recognize Saul's relationship with David in this psalm/song. Thoughts?

- As most people read the Bible in translation, can you see the nonsensical nature of the so-called "literal reading" of scripture?

Seven

Hebron

WITH THE DEATH OF Saul, it seems there is no impediment to the kingship of David—if only in Judah. So, David enquires of the Lord as to whether he should go up to one of the cities within Judah, and the Lord replies, "Hebron." So let us now transition to Hebron to see what transpires. It is without much ado that David is anointed king over Judah. Once more, you are right, Stranger. Judah is only a small portion of Israel. But there is a snag—as you shall see. First let us note that David's first act as king of Judah is to send messengers to Jabesh-Gilead in the Jordan valley of Israel, to thank the men there who had buried Saul. And see! He now commands his scribe to write that because the men of Jabesh-Gilead have shown *khesed* to Saul, may the Lord show them the same measure of *khesed*—adding that he, David, will deal favorably with them. But what he really wants them to know comes at the end of his missive, so mark this well. Listen! He reminds them that Saul is now dead and that Judah has anointed him as king. Clever—wouldn't you say? He doesn't come right out and say that the Lord, through Samuel, has anointed him king in Saul's stead. Rather, he leaves it for them to decide whether or not to accept David as king over all of Israel.

Oh—but you wish to know the meaning of the Hebrew word you heard: *khesed*. I am afraid I cannot adequately translate it. It is a quintessentially Hebrew word—one *feels* what it means rather than rationalizes it. In your translated scriptures, it usually requires two or more words, such as "covenant loyalty," "loving-kindness," "gracious mercy" or the like. It is expressive of the quality of friendship enjoyed by David and Jonathan—or Ruth and Naomi. If you have a best friend for whom you would do anything, you will understand. "Going the extra mile" counts as nothing.

So we see that David is offering this sort of friendship pact with the tribes of Israel, if they acknowledge his kingship. But here comes the snag. Abner, the commander of Saul's army, has survived the debacle at Mount Gilboa. He decides to appoint a surviving son of Saul, Ishba'al, as king over Israel. You might also know the king's name as Ishbosheth, which means "a man of shame" because his given name "Ishba'al" contains the name of the Canaanite god Ba'al. Thus, the scribes and redactors of our scriptures reflected their disdain for the Canaanite god by changing his name. And so, our tiny kingdom was divided—as it would be for most of its existence.

Gibeon

North of Jerusalem

This is where I come into the account, Stranger, so, you might as well see me in action. My brothers and I had been scouting out the land to the north of Jerusalem with a detachment of our army, when we came upon Abner and his men. Abner, as you might know, is the cousin of Saul. Thus, both armies are led by relatives of their respective king. As you can witness, we meet uneasily at the pool of Gibeon, where I concocted a plan, in the hope of breaking the stalemate between the kingdoms of Israel and Judah. I suggested that a dozen men from each army should have a contest, to exhibit their skills—except that I instructed our men to kill their opposite numbers in the contest. After all, my uncle had been anointed king over all Israel and Judah by the hand of Samuel. Ishba'al had no real claim to the throne. Whatever you might think of my decision and actions, remember that I have already faced judgment.

Yes, once more you see that this king-making is bloody business. With the killing of the twelve supporters of Ishba'al. Abner and the survivors flee; thus the real contest for the kingship of Israel has begun. But continue watching, Stranger, despite the pain it will bring me to see this again.

Mark there! My brother Asahel sets off fearlessly in pursuit of Abner. Abner recognizes my brother and entreats him to go after another soldier and take his spoil, but Asahel would not turn from his pursuit. Alas, he catches up with Abner, only to be run through with Abner's spear. To this day, it breaks my heart to remember it—but to see it for the first time, after all of these years . . . ah. I suppose my dear brother hoped we would rout the army of Israel by killing their commander—such things happened. In any case, it was his undoing, but take note of how all his fellow soldiers pause when they come upon his fallen body.

However, there remained a battle to be fought, so my remaining brother, Abishai, and I continued to pursue Abner and his army—after all, we now wanted to avenge our brother. Fortunately for Abner and his men, they find a hill upon which they can form a defensive perimeter. This provides a pause for both factions to let the blood cool from the exhausting business of battle. And it is Abner who causes all of us to reflect upon our actions. Hear him now: "Shall the sword continue to devour life? Surely you know this will come to a bitter end. When will you call off your men from pursuing their brothers?" Abner's words pierced my heart, for it was not only my brother who had died in battle, but also our fellow Israelites. And if the tale of Cain and Abel teaches us anything, it is that all murder is fratricide, for it is the same God who created us all. Thus, despite the hard fighting of the day, I sound the horn and lead my men on an overnight march back to our camp at Mahana'im. There we counted our losses before marching to Hebron to rejoin David.

And so we settled into a long war of attrition between the house of Saul and the house of David. There is no war so senseless as a civil war—one people as well as individual families divided. Alas, it is never so simple as one fracture within a society, but rather there are the continued aftershocks which multiply the divisions. This we will witness now in the household of Saul. As it was Abner, the power behind the throne, who put Ishba'al in the place of his father, Saul, so Abner arrogates to himself the perquisites of his power. In this case it is one of Saul's concubines, Rizpah. Ishba'al takes umbrage at the fact that Abner has had sexual relations with one of Saul's concubines, as they are now his. Ishba'al sees this as a liberty too far—a trespass upon his royalty prerogative. Ishba'al doesn't seem to realize that his kingship only exists because of Abner and the army. And so, as with most of humanity, he is the architect of his own undoing. Let us listen to Abner. "Am I a lackey for Judah? Here I am showing *khesed* to the household of your father, Saul, as well as to his brothers and his friends, and I have not turned you over to David. And yet today you hold me to account over a matter with a woman. May God do to Abner and more, if as the Lord has sworn to David, I do not accomplish it for him: to transfer the kingship from the house of Saul, and to set up the throne of David over Israel and Judah, from Dan to Be'er-sheba." The action between Ishba'al and Abner begs the question: *To whom* were the *people and soldiers* loyal? The narrative here leaves no doubt that the one perceived as a leader or strong man (in this case Abner), is the one to whom people will show allegiance. To put it crassly: most of us prefer to back a winner. How else could a commander tell his commander-in-chief, the *king*, that his dominion is his no longer? To do so, he must stand *de facto* as the *real power* in the kingdom.

Stranger, note how fear has gripped Ishba'al! Certainly, he must have known that his kingship was dependent upon Abner and the army—and that the army would be loyal to Abner. Of all the people he could have picked with which to flex his royal muscles, he had to choose Abner! This ironic twist only serves to show the extent to which Ishba'al is a puppet of Abner (not to mention God!). It also poses the question: Isn't it ironic that now Abner acknowledges David as the rightful king, "as the Lord has sworn to David," although he had thrown his lot in with Ishba'al? Does he think he can be David's master as well? Or perhaps he recognized that by my position as head of David's army, Abner knew his position would be lessened if he backed David as king? I do not know, and I have never asked him. The court journalist of the Samuel scrolls leaves a gap in the account and the answer lies ahead. See how easily kings are made and unmade! Stranger, I see you looking at me intently—and I sense your unspoken question, regarding me and king-making. Will you trust me that your question will be answered in the course of your visit? Fine.

What I know is that Abner set about bringing Ishba'al's kingship to an end. It is Abner who has made Ishba'al a king, and he is now about to dispose of that kingdom, which will in turn make the kingdom of David even greater. Is it not curious that Abner is experiencing no resistance from Ishba'al?

See now—Abner is sending messengers to David. Pay attention to the message! "To whom does the land belong? Make your pact with me and my power will be with you, to transfer all of the allegiance of Israel to you." Now we transition to David, who, upon receiving Abner's terms, agrees, but with one condition: Abner must bring to David Saul's daughter, Michal, to whom he was betrothed, for the price of many a Philistine foreskin. David is aware that by marrying Saul's daughter, he will have an air of legitimacy with the Israelites that he now lacks. After all, he is not lacking in wives; rather this is a way of consolidating his power. You might remember that Saul, although he had promised Michal to David, had given her in marriage to another man. So, David is also settling scores with the house of Saul, while at the same time becoming the departed Saul's son-in-law. My uncle was nothing if not shrewd!

Stranger, I hope these changes of place and time do not leave you exhausted or confused. No? That is good, for there is yet so much to see—and to learn. See, Abner has called a meeting with the elders of Israel—mark well what he says to them: "For some time now, you have been seeking David for king over you. Now do it! For the Lord has spoken to David, 'By the hand of my servant, David, I will save my people, Israel, from the hand of the Philistines and from all of their enemies.'"

Yes, you are right to query how anyone could trust a man who changes loyalty so quickly. For my part, I did not, as you will see. But for the moment, let us observe Abner's mission to David's camp. David warmly greets him and his detachment of bodyguards and orders that a feast be prepared for them. David's heart is light, for it looks as though the civil war is nearly at an end, because Abner promises to bring all of Israel into a covenant recognizing David as the legitimate king. When Abner departs, it is with contentment . . . and perhaps with a sense of self-satisfaction, for he has avenged himself against Ishba'al for the insult concerning the concubine. But what is more, in bringing down the kingship of Ishba'al, he feels he has as good as made the kingship of David over a united Israel. For my part, I can only conclude that David is the *passive recipient* of a now united kingdom. He only has to *accept the gift* made of Israel and to rule over both it and Judah. Has David won it through warfare or skilful diplomacy? No—rather, it has come to him through the *impotence* of a king, his opposite number: Ishba'al.

Hebron

Now, despite our war with Ishba'al, we had not ceased our raids on other tribes. There, see? I am returning with our soldiers from such an excursion. We can clearly see that there has been a feast, but there is also a commotion over the news which Abner delivered to David, as well as the fact that David had allowed Abner to depart in peace. Abner! He who had slain my brother, Asahel! You can see my reaction, Stranger, as the news is related to me. As I have indicated already, as a man of war I wasn't given to reflection—but to action. For good or for ill, it is the way I was. Although, like all of us here in life continuing, I have had many centuries to learn the art of reflection! Thus, I can watch and listen to myself in action with a measure of dispassion as I display my displeasure and anger with my uncle and king.

"What is this you have done? Abner came here? Why then did you send him away again? You know that Abner, son of Ner, came to deceive you—to discover your goings and comings and to learn all of your actions!" And see! I storm away without giving my king a chance to reply. Yes, I was impetuous in those days. What is more, I sent messengers after Abner to bring him back to Hebron—all without telling David. How could I get away with such actions? Your very question tells you something about how kings gain and retain power—only with the good graces of their armies. Abner and I had this in common: we enjoyed the loyalty of the men in our command. Keep this in mind as events unfold.

I cannot say I am proud of what you are about to witness. But if you are truly to learn about David, as he was, then the same must apply to me. Look yonder—Abner has returned to Hebron. I approach him as one commander to another and ask him to accompany me to the city gate, where matters were often discussed and adjudicated . . . and where justice was dispensed. Ah . . . you wince at the way I strike him down without mercy. Yes, from this point of view it seems a pointless waste. But the Joab you are watching still grieves his brother, Asahel, who died at the hands of Abner. My blood boiled for revenge. Yes, I struck him in the same way Asahel died—in the belly. But is it not still the same way amongst humanity—blood for blood? Why else is there war? Revenge is a contagion, Stranger, and sadly it is only exterminated when all blood has been spilt.

And David's response? It is forthcoming, only listen, he speaks now. "I and my kingdom are forever guiltless before the Lord, for the blood of Abner, son of Ner. May it be borne upon the head of Joab and all the house of his father, and may the house of Joab never be without someone who has a discharge of pus, or leprosy, or who needs crutches, or who falls by the sword or who goes hungry!"

Yes, Stranger, he not only cursed me, but all of my descendants as well—who are at the same time *his sister's* descendants, and thus David's relatives! And note in the scriptures that the court journalist also implicates my brother, Abishai, in the killing of Abner. He certainly didn't complain that I avenged our brother, but the guilt remains mine. Don't you wonder how David might have felt or what he might have done had Abner killed one of his brothers? In any event, Asahel was David's nephew! He should have welcomed Abner's death. But enough! And so, David commands me and all the rest of those at Hebron to mourn the death of Abner. As you can see, we had to tear our clothes and then put on sackcloth. Oh yes, I went along with it—a command is a command, but my heart was not in it. Many is the time I have wondered whether David's heart was truly in it. After all, he had everything to gain by his show of emotion and grief for the leader of the very army which sought to kill him—and the rest of us for that matter! What is the phrase you use today, Stranger?—"playing to the crowd"? Well, listen to David's last statement on the matter: "Do you not know that a great leader has fallen this day in Israel? And I am this day weak, though the anointed king. These men, the sons of Zeruiah, are too hard for me! May the Lord repay the evil doer according to his deed."

Stranger, I see the questions flooding from your eyes. Please, ask me! Why didn't David have me executed for what he saw as murder? He would have only created another blood feud. Remember, my brother Abishai would have avenged me. Yes, David could have dismissed me as head of his army, but how did such a reprimand work out for Ishba'al? In some ways, you could compare kingship and familial relationships in my earthly time to your mafia families today. Kill the wrong person and loyalties can quickly change. David knew that and admitted as much when he lamented: "These men, the sons of Zeruiah, are too hard for me!"

For consideration:

- David was no stranger to spilling blood. Why do you think he mourned the death of Abner, who stood between him and his divinely promised kingdom?

- How important a role does David's having been anointed play in the preceding events?

Eight

An Unpleasant Interlude

STRANGER, YOU HAVE SEEN how David killed the messenger who told him of the death of Saul and Jonathan at the hands of the Philistines. Being a messenger in my day was a risky business, and so it is in the next episode we are about to see. As you know, Abner promised to help David secure the whole of Israel for his kingdom but died before being able to carry out his promise. When Abner's death became known, Israel was thrown into turmoil. Such is an opportune time for those who wish to advance their positions in life—particularly with a new king such as David. The men I have in mind are two brothers, Ba'anah and Rechab, both of whom had commanded raiding parties under King Saul. With David's rising power and Ishba'al's relative weakness, these brothers see their chance to impress David. Let us follow their action.

Be prepared, Stranger, for like David's raids against the tribes of southern Judah, Ba'anah and Rechab are used to dealing in blood. See—the sun is at its height. Not a time for those with privilege to be out or doing business. And so it is with Ishba'al; he is taking what you might call a "siesta." As officers in Saul's army, Ba'anah and Rechab would have been familiar figures amongst the king's staff, so they are not seen as suspicious when they make their way into the king's household. We can follow them as they make their way into the king's bedchamber. For these two men, killing is an everyday matter, and so they dispatch their weakling king with a sword thrust to the belly. Do you feel ill, Stranger? I thought you knew they were going to behead Ishba‘al as well—it's all in the scriptures. In any case, it's much easier to carry a man's head as proof of his death than his entire body—even if he were a king. They spirit poor Ishba‘al's head out of the palace and ride day and night to David at Hebron. Happily, you and I can make this journey in an instant. Look yonder—they are approaching David. Perhaps, while travelling, they have discussed how David might reward them for removing this stumbling block between him and kingship over a united Israel? Why wouldn't they, as Abner is no longer around to fulfil his pledge to David to bring all of Israel over to David?

But brace yourself, Stranger, you are about to witness vintage David. Look, it is with supreme confidence the brothers approach David. And it is without any formalities they announce and present their "gift" to him.

"Here is the head of Ishba‘al, Saul's son, your enemy who sought your life! The Lord has given to my lord the king vengeance this day on Saul and his offspring!"

Mind you, Stranger, the average man who lusts for power would have welcomed this news and proof that his enemy was dead—but not David. As you can see, my uncle welcomes this news no more than when I killed Abner, who had not only led Ishba‘al's army against David—and all of us—but also killed my brother, David's nephew. Instead, he orders his young men not only to kill Ba‘anah and Rechab, but to mutilate their bodies, and hang what's left by the pool in Hebron. Such treatment of corpses is a display of utter contempt for the individuals. And you are right, Stranger, such atrocities did not cease in ancient times, but have continued at public places such as Traitors' Gate in London, with prisoners' heads on pikes or, more publicly in your time, with videos posted by jihadis. As for me, apart from Abner, I killed men in battle. I had no need to lord it over their dead bodies, for I knew it could just as easily have been myself lying there. But my uncle, alas, had an almost vicious streak that showed itself from time to time. I cannot say I always felt comfortable in his presence. Saul had his moods, certainly, but David's heart hardened without warning.

Think back over what you have just witnessed, Stranger. Do you not, once again, find a sense of irony in what has transpired? Ah—very good! Yes, both Rechab and Ba'anah tell David that they are only accepting what the Lord has spoken to him through Samuel. Whether they have helped David's ascent to the kingship over all Israel for selfish reasons or simply as their acceptance of the inevitable is immaterial. In fact, what they have done accords with the Lord's promise to David. So, in at least one aspect, what they have said to David was in fact the truth! But for reasons known only to David, he will not brook any violence against the family of Saul, Israel's disgraced and defunct king. And so Ishba'al's head is buried with the remains of Abner, his former commander of the army. Enough of this bloodshed—at least for now—we shall now witness happier scenes.

For consideration:

- As a long-time teacher of Hebrew Bible, I can attest that too many people only remember David as the killer of Goliath and writer of psalms. Has your view of David been challenged by this book? Have you re-read the books of Samuel?
- Were Ba'anah and Rechab un/justly killed by David?

Nine

Hebron

David Becomes King over all Israel/Judah

YES, STRANGER, WE ARE still in Hebron. The gathering you see before you is comprised of the elders and representatives of all the tribes of Israel and Judah. David is making his covenant with them. After all we have witnessed, it is rather anti-climactic, is it not? You are astute to ask, Stranger, for why indeed does David need to make a covenant with those tribes which fought against him, especially when it is the Lord who has chosen David as king? Perhaps it is to ratify a decision which was made in heaven? Frankly, I don't know. Why look at me that way? Being here in life continuing does not confer one with the full knowledge of our Creator. But look! They are anointing David king—yes, again! It sounds like the beginning of a joke: how many anointings does it take to make a king over Israel! Ha! Jewish humor goes back a long way.

Jerusalem and the Ark of the Covenant

Now David needs a city from which to rule over the united Israel; and the only one which suits his needs is Jerusalem. The problem is that it already has inhabitants—the Jebusites. I won't bore you with the details of its capture, for in fact, it was I and a group of hand-picked soldiers who made the assault. We entered the city the same way as did their life-giving water during a siege—through the underground water shaft! Homer's Greeks were not the only ones to use such a small force to bring about the fall of a great city. But were we more sparing of the Jebusites than the Greeks were of Troy's inhabitants? Sadly, slaughter is too often the way of dispossessing people of their inheritance. We Hebrews experienced it as well—at the hands of the Assyrians, Babylonians, Greeks, and Romans—to name only a few. Such is the way of human society.

Once David consolidates his power over the united Israel and establishes himself in Jerusalem, he comes to the attention of Hiram, the king of Tyre in Lebanon, our neighbor to the north. David avails himself of the craftsmen and fine cedar wood made available by Hiram. This is as good as a treaty of non-aggression between the Israel's new king and the more established kingdom to the north. And, having built himself a fine palace, David does what any potentate does: he takes more wives and concubines and fills his palace with children! I came to have more aunts and cousins than I could count.

As news of David's kingship spreads, it is not long before the Philistines, with whom David not only took refuge, but also served, come to understand that David's loyalty was *self*-serving. Thus, warfare becomes inevitable. What follows—and I trust we need not observe them, Stranger, is a series of battles in which David is victorious. The question remains: had David been honest when he pledged his loyalty to the Philistine king, Achish, when he and his men took refuge in Ziklag, or was his "loyalty" simply a matter of expedience? I was in no position of authority then, so I cannot say. But certainly, those who are supporters of the legend of David would contend that he was clever and managed to deceive the Philistines by playing them against Saul. The Philistines, as you might assume, would see his betrayal differently. No one really likes a turncoat.

Let us now observe David at what I believe is the zenith of his reign as king. Having made Jerusalem his political capital, David now seeks to establish it as the center of worship, by bringing the ark of the covenant there. Stranger, we will let the scribes and scholars debate where the ark was at this point in time, but between you and me, I say it was at Kireath-jearim, for that is where I am taking us.

See how David has assembled his mighty warriors for this occasion. A new cart has been fashioned on which to transport this most holy object in all Israel to Jerusalem. There are music, celebration and dancing to mark the occasion. Mind you, some bizarre things happen while the ark is en route to Jerusalem—which are not our focus—so suffice it to say the ark is left at the farm of a Philistine, Obed-edom, for the time being. This being just one of several strange aspects of the ark's journey. However, as David is our focus, let us concentrate on him.

Once more, we hear music and see people dancing in celebration of the ark's arrival in Jerusalem. There is David whirling about with abandon and wearing only a linen ephod (revealing more than concealing)! The ephod is normally an item of clothing worn by Israel's priests. Yet today, David is both king and priest rolled into one, and so he celebrates. However, someone who is not celebrating is Michal, David's wife and daughter of Saul. She is observing the festivities from the palace. Take note of her mirthless face. Again, Stranger, your questions are apt: Was she ordered by David to stay in the palace, or has she chosen to remain there? You would have to seek her out here in life continuing to know the answer. But in any case, she keeps her counsel—if only for now. Meanwhile David has the ark placed within the tent he has erected for it and goes about offering sacrifices to the Lord and blessing his people. As befits such a celebration, David distributes food to all the gathered throng.

As the public festivities come to an end, David goes to bless his household, but see!—before he can do so, he is met by Michal, who is not in a festive mood. Let's listen.

"My, how the king of Israel has honored himself today—uncovering himself in full view of his servants' maids! Just like one of the perverts exposes himself!"

It is good to remember, Stranger, that Michal is not only David's wife, but she is also the daughter of Israel's first king and knows something of royal decorum. Furthermore, she loved David to the extent that she defied her father and helped David escape Saul, when he wanted to kill David. Neither should we forget that her father, Saul, was punished by the Lord for usurping the role of priest. Yet here is David doing as he likes. Poor Michal must have had conflicted feelings regarding David, but as to her true motivations for excoriating him, alas, no one can know the thoughts of another; we can only see the actions proceeding from that person. If Michal thought to sting David's pride or "bring him to his senses," she has sadly misjudged her husband. After all, for David, she is simply one wife among many. Listen for yourself, as David has the last word.

"The Lord has chosen me over your father and all of his household, to appoint me as prince over his people, over Israel; thus, I will celebrate before the Lord. I will make myself an even greater object of ridicule, abased in my own eyes and, as for the maids whom you mentioned, I shall be honored!"

There, Stranger, you have witnessed the effective end of the marriage between David and Michal. She who saved her husband's life at the risk of her own, will no longer produce life, as her husband will, from this moment, only turn to his other wives and concubines. You need to understand that this was a cruel punishment in its day. I understand it is no longer the case in the society from which you come, Stranger. But for a woman, who is also a princess, it was a death sentence, watching the other women in the king's harem becoming pregnant. So, as you see, my uncle had a cruel streak . . . and sadly, more is to come. Yes, he seems to have overtones of Saul. Saul had his radical mood shifts; but so too has David, in his own way: ecstatic joy over the ark's entry into Jerusalem turned quickly to vicious vindictiveness with Michal.

For consideration:

- Was the ark's journey to Jerusalem more about God or David?
- Put yourself in Michal's shoes. Was she right to chide David? Was David's punishment of Michal justifiable or simply cruel?

Ten

Jerusalem

AND NOW I WANT to take us forward in time—which is only possible here in life continuing because there is no time!—for I am sensing that you have no need to witness how David conquered neighboring territories and took tribute from them. He simply behaved as any person with absolute power behaves—kind to his friends and ruthless toward his enemies. Thus, having extended and secured the borders of his kingdom, David is feeling magnanimous and enquires whether there is anyone left from the household of Saul to whom he can show *khesed*, for the sake of his departed best friend, Jonathan. Yes, it's that Hebrew word again which is impossible to translate. *Khesed* is always best understood in action.

Some of David's courtiers know there remains a former servant from Saul's household called Ziba, so they call him to David. Let's listen. Ziba now stands before the king.

"You are Ziba?"

"Your servant."

"Is there still someone from the house of Saul for whom I may show the *khesed* of God?"

"There is a son of Jonathan; he is lame in both feet."

"Where is he?"

"He is in the house of Machir, son of Ammiel, in Lo-debar."

So, David sends forth his servants to fetch Meriba'al to his palace in Jerusalem. What is that, Stranger? You have read his name also as Mephibosheth? Yes, it is the same case as with Ishba'al. You might recall what I mentioned to you previously about our scribes' taking liberties with earlier texts. So, if they felt a name might contain the name of a Canaanite deity, such as "Ba'al," then they changed it. So because Meriba'al means "one who strives for Ba'al," the scribal emendation renders his name Mephibosheth, which means "one who spreads shame." In other words, he is shameful for worshiping or serving a god other than the God of Israel. Yes, when reading the Hebrew scriptures, not all is as it first appears. And to read them *only in translation*—don't get me started! It requires that one read behind the text, as it were. Yes, I understand, Stranger, yet here in life continuing we recognize that people on the earth want easy answers and cannot handle shades of gray in a world which prefers black and white—particularly when it comes to belief systems. Most of us have been guilty of it at some point in our incarnations. It causes untold misery and unnecessary suffering on earth, when everyone has the need to be right or to have exclusive access to the truth. Most of life on earth is spent like the parable of the blind men describing an elephant to each other! Ironic, is it not, that in so many myths, poems and epics, we here in life continuing are described as "shades" who long to return to our incarnation of the past! Nothing could be further from the truth— for it is here that we see and understand most clearly. Yours will be a heavy burden when you return to your life; after all, who will be inclined to believe anything you tell them? I fear you too will have to write your own epic and leave it to others to recognize its veracity for themselves! But let us return to David and Meriba'al, as the latter now stands before his king.

As with Ziba, Meriba'al stands in fear before David, for he understands how precariously his life hangs in the balance. Why wouldn't David want to kill any remaining heirs of King Saul? As is custom, the king speaks first.

"Meriba'al." Note, Stranger, David does not address Meriba'al with a greeting of peace or a blessing—this adds to Meriba'al's discomfort.

"Your servant is here before you."

"You have no reason to fear, for I am going to treat you with *khesed* for the sake of Jonathan, your father. I will restore to you all of the land of Saul, your father. And you shall always eat your meals at my table."

"What is your servant that you should take note of a dead dog like me?"

As you can see for yourself, Stranger, David does not answer Meriba'al's question. Instead, he calls for Ziba to be brought before him again.

"Everything that belonged to Saul and to his entire household I now give to your lord's son. And you, your sons, and your servants shall work the land for him; and you shall bring the produce to the son of your lord, Meriba'al, the son of your lord shall always take his meals at my table."

What is that, Stranger? Why does David repeat that Meriba'al shall always take his meals at the king's table? Perhaps you should tell me as I can already sense your thoughts. Ah yes, David's *khesed* could well be interpreted as keeping his friends close and his enemies closer. After all, the only ostensible male left from the lineage of Saul is Meriba'al—as well as his young son. Meriba'al, being lame, can hardly lead an insurrection against David. Mica, his son, is another matter. But as their meals will always be taken at the king's table, there will always be many eyes and ears to keep account of them in the event they should consider a rebellion. As you see life from this side of the veil between life and death, you are beginning to understand how so many human gestures—however magnanimous they might first appear—often have mixed motives lying behind them. Our conversation brings to mind Machiavelli—I think you would find him a most entertaining spirit with whom you might converse. He's not quite the cynic as some would believe—only consider our subject David! And with that said, I fear it is time to turn to a most sordid affair, in which I played no little part.

For consideration:

- During my ministry I have worked with Christians who truly believed the King James Version of the Bible was the "original" Bible, and not a translation from 1611. Have you encountered such opinions? How did you handle them?

- There is also a mistaken notion that once the scriptures were written, they remained henceforth untouched. Yet it is well known that there are varying versions of the biblical books. For some this is a major problem; for others it is a fascinating fact in the Bible's development. Where do you stand and why?

- When the Bible is not properly understood, it can become a dangerous weapon. We can see too many such examples in our time.

Eleven

Joab to the Battle Front
Ammon

Now, MY VISITOR, WE come to a point in your visit—and in the life of David—wherein I play a larger role. But I feel it is necessary that you should see my actions as they interrelate to David's. Be warned, the coming episodes will warrant your closest attention. So much of David's fate—and mine—are affected by what you will hear and see.

As for what you are about to witness, the kingdom of Ammon is directly across the Jordan valley from Jerusalem. Both of these cities are perched high in the rugged hills overlooking the deep rift below. At this point in time, Ammon's king, Nakhash, has died and is succeeded by his son, Khanun. You might find their names somewhat amusing when translated into your tongue. The dead monarch's name, Nakhash, means "serpent" or "snake." Khanun might be translated as "favored one." We shall follow David's envoys to Ammon, for by their hand David will send his condolences to Khanun on the death of his father. It's a generous gesture from Israel toward a country between whom no love was lost.

Note how David's messengers are received in Ammon—there is suspicion and hesitancy to take them at their word. Hear what the chiefs among the people have to say to their king. "Is it to honor your father in your eyes that David has sent comforters to you? Isn't it rather to scope out and spy upon the city so he might overthrow it, that David has sent his servants to you?" Khanun accepts the advice of his chieftains and has David's envoys publicly disgraced—first by having half of their beards shaved off and then by having their garments cut off at the waist, thereby exposing their genitals. It is in such condition that these men must make their way back to Israelite territory—much to the amusement of the Ammonites. However, as you can see, the humiliation of these ambassadors is matched only by the outrage shown by David upon their return. And thus begins the war between Israel and Ammon.

Khanun belatedly realized the offense he had caused his near—and stronger—neighbor, so he set about hiring mercenaries from Syria. I was sent at the head of Israel's army to attack Ammon. Although we were the better fighting force, it became clear to me that we were outnumbered by our enemies. The Syrian mercenaries remained in the open field while the Ammonites drew up in formation just outside the city gates—leaving themselves an escape to the safety inside the city walls, should it be necessary. I often wondered what the Syrians thought about that. Seeing that my forces were positioned between the two, I took the risky decision of dividing our men into two groups. Yes, you are right, Stranger—it is always a risk to divide one's forces when in enemy territory. But David had put me in command and trusted me to do what was best. I selected a handpicked group of men I knew I could trust to help me face the Syrians. The remainder of our soldiers I put under the command of my brother, Abishai, to deal with the Ammonites. My brother and I had a simple plan: whoever became the more hard-pressed in the coming battle, the other would come to his aid. And what if both of our forces were equally hard-pressed? Good question! For my answer, listen to what I said to Abishai all those years ago: "Let us be courageous for the sake of our people and for the sake of the cities of our God and may the Lord do what seems best in his eyes."

Ah, you note that I did not pray for victory. Certainly, I hoped we would win, but as a seasoned warrior, I also know that battles can turn on the slightest decision. Ultimately, I knew then—as I certainly know now—that my life has never been fully under my control. Only those inexperienced in warfare think otherwise.

However, as the British special forces motto reads: "Who dares wins." In this instance I dare, and the Syrians flee in the face of our assault. That puts paid to the courage of the Ammonites as well, for see—they can't get inside the city walls fast enough! What a disaster for us! You ask *why a disaster*? Because now it means siege warfare—which is long, tedious and costly. It takes the fighting edge off the men; it means scavenging for food in a foreign land, keeping up morale and the persistent danger of disease breaking out in the camp. Win or lose, a short, sharp engagement is to be preferred to a siege. In the event, I decided to leave the army encamped around Ammon and returned to Jerusalem to report to David.

The Syrians, having come off the worse for the alliance with Ammon, withdrew within their borders, no doubt licking their wounds. As you might guess, their king, Hadadezer, was not pleased by the performance of his troops in the face of Israel, so he called upon neighboring forces to join him in a combined attack against the upstart king, David. Do you fancy observing more ancient warfare, Stranger? I thought not. Except for those involved in the fighting—and in particular those who survived the slaughter and have made something of a name for themselves—warfare is both disgusting and tedious. Suffice it to say, David gathered all of the fighting men of Israel and went out against Hadadezer at the head of his army. David was, of course, victorious, so all of the petty kingdoms who had joined Hadadezer in his vain attempt to save face became subject to Israel and paid David tribute. As you might assume, my uncle was full of himself. But as one of our wise Hebrew poets has written: "Arrogance precedes ruination." And if you know anything about David, you will know exactly to what I am referring.

For consideration:

- Does the reaction of the Ammonites to David's emissaries bring to mind Abner's approach to David?

Twelve

Jerusalem and Bathsheba
or
I Wonder What the King is Doing Tonight

AT THIS POINT IN your visit, we must first look at the written account of what we are about to witness. And here it is! Ha! I, too, remember my initial amazement at how quickly things appear and disappear here in life continuing. Now, Stranger, we will read from the beginning of what you would call Chapter Eleven of the second scroll of Samuel. Let me be clear . . . without taking a close look at the text, it will be easy for you to fall into the trap of the David legend, as opposed to the actual doings of the man himself. We will concentrate on the first verse, as the rest of David's life turns upon it.

"At the turn of the year, when kings go forth, David sent Joab and his servants with him—and all Israel—and they ravaged the Ammonites and besieged Rabbah. But David remained in Jerusalem."

I fear we shall linger over these words for some time. Moreover, we will need to take a look at the original Hebrew text as written by the court journalist. But first, please let your eyes adjust to the Hebrew text and soon its meaning will appear to you. Note that our scribes did not have vowel letters in their alphabet. Yes, you heard me correctly—no vowels . . . They could use some letters of the Hebrew alphabet to express vowels, but only in specific cases. Please bear with me, my visitor—for I have much to explain.

The Hebrew word for "king" is *melek*, so if we take out the vowels, we are left only with the consonantal letters: *mlk*. Next, the plural for kings is *mlkim*. In this case, the Hebrew script allows a vowel only for "i." Now, I want you to note how "kings" is written in our case here: *mlakim*, with an extra letter "a" that seems unwarranted in this case. Many rabbis and scholars contend that this spelling was simply a mistake, but—as I was there—I am not so certain. (You can make up your own mind.) For the moment, hold on to this so-called misspelling of "kings" and let me ask your opinion. Does anything strike you as odd—or even ironic—about this first verse? Take your time. Read the verse again. Indeed! When "kings go forth," David—Israel's king of kings *par excellence*—remains in Jerusalem. Note that the court journalist doesn't directly criticize David. How could he keep his job—not to mention his head—if he did so? Rather, he adopts an impassive tone, leaving hints, gaps in information, unresolved inconsistencies, etc. for the discerning reader to piece together. The court journalist has found such a reader in you.

So let us now once more observe my uncle, the king. While remaining at home, David strolls upon the roof of his royal residence and happens to notice a neighbor, Bathsheba, bathing in a nearby house. David is taken in by her beauty and doubtlessly her nudity—but rather than turning to one of his wives or concubines to satisfy his sexual urge—David enquires about her from his servants. The response we hear is almost matter-of-fact, as though David should know this information. "Is this not Bathsheba, the daughter of Eliam, the wife of Uriah the Hittite?" But see, David ignores the latter identification, that this woman is married. Rather, he calls for his servants and sends "messengers" to go and fetch her for him.

Now, Stranger, here is where the word I asked you to remember, *mlakim*—or "kings"—comes into play. This spelling is normally used for the word *mlakim*, which in the Hebrew of my time meant "messengers." Yes, "messengers," the very word used when the text mentions David's sending messengers to bring Bathsheba over to him. But in this account of David's transgression, *mlakim/* messengers looks like *mlakim/*kings. So, what do you think: is it an accidental or deliberate wordplay—or is it perhaps what you today might call a "Freudian slip?" Whether or not the pun is intentional, the irony is patently clear! While his army ravages the Ammonites, David ravages Bathsheba; and while the fate of besieged Rabbah hangs in the balance, so do the marriage and life of Uriah. . .as well as the fate of the house of David.

You know, Stranger, many are those who see David's ravaging of Bathsheba as some sort of romantic liaison. But romance only works between equals. David didn't pitch up at her doorstep with wine and flowers, telling her that he had espied her from afar and couldn't stop thinking about her. No. As you witnessed, he sent his men—*mlakim/*messengers—to bring her forcibly to him. This wasn't an invitation, but a royal command. I think this is why the court journalist put no words into Bathsheba's mouth. How could he have done so? Had he included her cries and pleas, this account would never have been written. Why do I say this? Again, look at your world today. How many world leaders let secretaries or aides expose their indiscretions or crimes—*and keep their jobs*, as well as their lives? What is missing from the court journalist's account are explicit value judgments and incriminating facts—such as motives: Why did David remain in Jerusalem? Is David in love with this creature he espies or is it simply lust? Doesn't David know he's breaking the seventh commandment: Do not commit adultery? You see, this absence of value judgments in the account is one of the features that produces the impression of the court journalist's seeming objectivity as regards David. "Just reporting the facts." However, my visitor, very soon you will witness a woman who will use her voice and thereby condemn not only her assailant but give voice to her sister, Bathsheba, as well.

As for Bathsheba's "voice" within the scroll, note that it only comes when she tells David "I am pregnant." These words galvanize David into action. To my embarrassment, Stranger, here is where I become enmeshed in this sordid affair. Look, even now you can see David hastily writing a message to me, while I am at the head of our army, fighting the Ammonites. All it says is: "Send me Uriah the Hittite." Note my perplexity as I receive and read the message. What could I do except obey my king's orders? At the time, I simply assumed my uncle had his reasons. Ah, my visitor, too much of life on earth is understood only long after the fact. What has my uncle learned since then? You ask such delving questions—but only he can answer that. Yes, I have spent time with him here in life continuing. As you are learning, one only need think about someone—or a specific time—to find oneself in the presence of that person or event. But truthfully, I have stopped wondering about my past, and now seek to learn about the other more fascinating lives that have been lived.

In any case, David, once a strong warrior and leader, now appears indolent, selfish and spoilt. As we have seen, David has *passively* received the gift of a united kingdom; now he is *actively* bringing about his own decline. For, ironically, it is this very activity through which David carefully orchestrates the trespasses, which will become for him a curse upon his house and lineage. There is no one or nothing else to blame.

Now that he has arrived in Jerusalem, see how puzzled Uriah is to have received the summons from David. The royal palace was close enough to Uriah's home for David to spy upon his wife, but not close enough for David to learn the name or common humanity of the man he has wronged—not to mention his wife, Bathsheba. David seeks to put Uriah at ease by asking about how I am faring, as well as our soldiers. Then he asks about the state of the war. Uriah trusts his king and perhaps feels honored that he has been asked to bring this situation report to David. David presents his loyal servant with a furlough. He tells Uriah to go down to his home and wash. He also gives Uriah some sort of trinket as a reward for bringing news from the battlefront. (By the way, Stranger, the scribes have written that David told Uriah to "wash his feet." Yes, foot-washing plays an important part of life in a dusty land; but "feet" is our prudish scribes' way of referring to genitalia! So there is a hint for Uriah to enjoy sex with Bathsheba contained in this statement.) Yet watch! Uriah simply goes out of the king's presence and makes his bed with the royal guards. This is then reported to David. Trying his best to sound magnanimous, we hear David cajoling Uriah. "Haven't you come from a journey? Why didn't you go down to your house?" Of course, what David probably wants to ask is, "Why didn't you sleep with your wife?"

Uriah's response to his king is telling. "The ark and Israel and Judah are sleeping in lean-tos in the open field. Should I then go to my home, eat and drink, and sleep with my wife? On my life, as well as yours, I will not do it!" What a way to speak to one's king! Did Uriah have suspicions as regards David and Bathsheba? Again, I can't say. But as David had sent more than one of his servants to have Bathsheba brought to him . . . well, who can say? Forgive me, Stranger, but all of this needs some further picking apart. Reading these scriptures only in translation leaves many of the deeper meanings hidden from view, like buried treasure. Here's what I mean. What is the name of Bathsheba's husband? Don't look at me that way! It's a simple question. Uriah the Hittite, you say? No. His name is Uriah, which means "the light of Yahweh," the Hebrews' name for God. But Uriah obviously comes from the lineage of another people: the Hittites. In any case, Uriah is indeed a Hebrew name. However, who would you say is living according to the light of God at this moment in time? The Hebrew king, David, or the "Hittite" soldier, Uriah? But let us continue our observations.

David is becoming more desperate to manipulate Uriah's behaviour in order to exonerate himself. Look. He's ordering Uriah to remain one more day in Jerusalem. Uriah shows as much meticulousness in his identification with the privations of David's army as does David in the enactment and concealment of his sin.

In an almost avuncular way—and I should know!—David wines and dines Uriah. In particular, he *wines* Uriah—to the point of drunkenness. Hoping that Uriah's mind and senses are sufficiently dimmed by the wine, David sends him to his home. But again, see how Uriah will have nothing to do with the king's scheme. Perhaps he truly knows nothing of David's rape of his wife. But as a soldier who is loyal to his God, his wife and king,

Uriah is also loyal to his comrades-in-arms. If they are roughing it, then how can he indulge in the pleasure denied to them? So once more, Uriah sleeps alongside the king's guardians. David's attempt to cover his sin is foiled—by his blameless servant.

Now you can witness the actions of a truly desperate man, for even David knows he is not above God's laws. At this point, it is the morning of Uriah's departure for the war against Ammon. In a nonchalant way, David asks Uriah to carry a message to Joab for him. Let us see what David writes. "Position Uriah at the front of the hardest fighting, then retreat, leaving him to be struck down and killed." David writes Uriah's death sentence and sends it to me via Uriah's own hand! This is my uncle at his most cynical and despotic behaviour; and again, on whom does David call to see to it that the sentence is carried out but his nephew Joab? Yes, I, Joab! The self-same Joab whom David cursed for the murder of Abner! Now he uses me as the instrument for the curse which will fall upon his house! More than a little ironic, wouldn't you say?

And so, the loyal Uriah carries his death warrant safely to my hands. Look, I even peruse the message in Uriah's presence, for I have no knowledge of its contents! Note my discomfort. How was I to know what the message contained? As the day was already far spent, I decide to delay Uriah's death until the morrow and send him to join his soldiers. See how I pace and worry. How to execute David's plan? Certainly, others will die as well—and these are all good men. I know them, for heaven's sake! But my uncle is king and as such, he can be generous with the blood of others! Tell me, Stranger, have you any need to see this shameful deed carried out? No? I thank you. Even after all this time, it still shames me and breaks my heart that I followed such an immoral order. What else could I have done, you ask? I could have filled a purse with money and told Uriah to desert. Perhaps I could have sent word to his wife to join him wherever he chose to hide. I could have secretly reported him dead to David. But, as you and history know, I did no such thing. I carried out a dastardly order. And for that, I carry the blame. Too often in life we tell ourselves that we have no real choice—that others might have free will, but that our actions are determined. Of course, this is one of those convenient lies we tell ourselves in order to comfort ourselves and to avoid living into our full humanity, which means living lives of compassion and truth. Most of us learn this lesson belatedly.

After Uriah's death, I must send a return message to David. I even go so far as to devise a "script" for the messenger. He must have thought me more than a little mad! Hear what I have to say.

"If David should become angry and ask you, 'Why did you draw so near to the city to fight? Surely you knew they would shoot from the walls. Who killed Abimelech, the son of Jerubesheth? Wasn't it a woman who threw a piece of a millstone from the wall, and he died at Thebez? Why did you approach so close to the wall?'"

"Then you shall say: 'Your servant Uriah is also dead.'" And so the messenger departs to convey my report to David. "Our adversaries grew too strong for us, as they were reinforced in the field from those within the walls. But we held them at the gate. And their archers shot at your servants from the walls and a number of your servants died—Uriah the Hittite was also among them." Let us note the king's reaction after my messenger reports to him. "Tell this to Joab: 'Don't let this matter trouble you; the sword claims this one and that one. Strengthen your attack on the city and capture it'... and encourage him." So, Stranger, you know what happens next. Yes, indeed. Bathsheba is informed of Uriah's death. Although the court journalist does not tell us her reaction—apart from going into mourning for her husband—can there be any doubt in her mind who arranged for Uriah's "convenient" disappearance? For no sooner than a suitable period of mourning is completed than David once more "sends" for Bathsheba and has her brought to his household to become one of his many wives. There she can carry her infant to full term without the prying eyes of suspicious neighbors or concerned family. But let's look at the Hebrew text to see how this sordid affair is summarized. "And the thing that David did was displeasing in the eyes of the Lord." How do some English-speakers put it? "No shit, Sherlock!" Anyone with the slightest familiarity with the Ten Commandments knows that adultery, lying and murder are forbidden! But how else could the court journalist record these events except with understatement? In addition, rather than rendering judgment on David himself, the court journalist puts the judgment within the province of the divine. Who can argue with that?

For consideration:

- Had you ever considered that literary devices, such as irony (or humor, etc.), were used in scripture? Should we be surprised to discover carefully crafted accounts, as it was our forebears who gave us literature and narrative technique?

- The use and abuse of women is as old as history. Would David be a candidate for today's #MeToo movement?

Thirteen

David is Judged

As MUCH AS MY uncle might have wanted to move on from his squalid actions concerning Bathsheba and Uriah, God had other ideas. Whereas David's previous activity has been denoted by his "sending" of henchmen, messengers, messages, myself, and more; God now does some divine "sending" in the form of the prophet Nathan. Nathan appears before David and tells him a little tale. Let's listen.

"Two men lived in a certain city; one was rich, the other poor. The wealthy man had a great number of flocks and herds. But as for the poor man, he had only one little ewe lamb which he had bought. And he raised it and she grew up along with him and his children. And she ate from his portion and drank from his cup, and she took her rest in his bosom, for she was like a daughter to him. Well, there came a traveller to the rich man, but he refused to take an animal from his flocks or herds to prepare for the visitor. Instead, he took the ewe lamb of the poor man and prepared it for his guest."

Now wait for David's reaction. See his righteous anger for this wrongdoing and hear his condemnation: "As the Lord lives, the man who did this deserves to die! And as for the lamb, he should repay fourfold for having done this thing and because he refused to show compassion!" And Nathan's response?

"You are the man!" In Hebrew, Nathan's response is encompassed in two short words. Perhaps the shortest judgment in the

Scriptures. But Nathan has more to say, for it is God's judgment which he has pronounced. Now comes God's reasoning.

"I anointed you as king over Israel and I rescued you from the hand of Saul. I gave you the house of your lord, Saul, and I gave his wives into your possession. I also gave you the house of Israel and Judah, and, as if this weren't enough, I was willing to add even more. So why have you so despised the word of the Lord that you have committed this sinful act against Uriah the Hittite? You have had him killed in battle with the Ammonites in order to take his wife for your own. Now the sword will never depart from your house, because you have scorned me and have taken the wife of Uriah the Hittite as your own. Therefore, I am raising up evil from within your own household. I will take your wives from before your eyes and give them to someone close to you. And he shall bed your wives in broad daylight. Whereas you have acted secretly, I shall do this thing before all Israel and in broad daylight!"

David has fallen into the trap of his own making, has he not? Struck to the core by God's judgment through Nathan, David now responds.

"I have sinned against the Lord."

What else can David say, Stranger? He couldn't manipulate Uriah, so, he can't hope to manipulate God. But hear what Nathan says next, for the Lord treats David differently from Saul.

"The Lord has set aside your sin, so you shall not die. However, the child born to you shall die."

One can certainly see how people can get the notion of a cruel God. Why the child and not David? And yes, yes, there is that phrase about the sins of the fathers being visited upon the children and the grandchildren. On earth and in time-bound existence, such thinking is far from satisfying . . . and appears to be downright unfair, does it not? I certainly had a sense of injustice about it all—particularly as I was an agent of David's crimes. You, my visitor, inhabit a world of quantum physics and randomness, whereas when I walked the earth, negative incidents and accidental death were often understood as God's disfavor. There is a popular phrase in today's English: "Shit happens." I suppose that adequately simplifies it! In any case, from here it all looks so very different . . . not right or better, just different. The visceral power of emotions plays no part. I have even met men whom I killed—such as Abner—but now there is no animosity, but only an understanding that is born of our common life in the source of our being.

Let us return to my uncle and king. The child to whom Bathsheba has given birth is gravely ill. Note how overwrought is David. Despite the dire prophecy from Nathan, David prays to God to spare the child. He fasts, he sleeps on the ground, abasing himself for the sake of this young life, which is so much more precious to him than the lives of Uriah and so many others. Perhaps this is because the child is innocent—just as was Uriah—and David must watch him die, unlike the blind eye David turned toward Uriah and the soldiers who died with him. Still, this tiny child becomes yet another victim of David's sin.

Now note my uncle's pragmatism upon learning of the child's death. He raises himself up from the earth, washes and anoints himself, goes to make an act of worship and then settles down to a nice meal. Only see how confused his servants are as they ask him:

"What is this thing you have done? While the child was living, you fasted and wept. Now that the child has died, you arise and eat." Of course, they assume that fasting is for the time of mourning. And David's response?

"While the child was yet alive, I fasted and wept, for I thought: 'Who knows whether the child might live?' But now he is dead, why should I fast? Am I able to bring him back again? I can go to him, but he shall not return to me."

What the court journalist next relates is probably known to you, Stranger. David "comforts" Bathsheba by having sexual relations with her. You are right to smirk and roll your eyes. It might have been a "comfort" to David, but the court journalist's stylus is silent as regards Bathsheba's needs. But we are quickly informed that the son born to them is called Solomon and that the Lord loved him. This latter piece of information is reinforced by God's sending once more the prophet Nathan, who calls the child Jedidiah, which is Hebrew for "beloved of the Lord." And yes, Solomon does become king after David's death, but only because of the misery and bloodshed which follow.

Meanwhile, I, of course, continued to ply my soldier's trade fighting the Ammonites while our army besieged Rabbah. Once we had captured their water supply, clearly it was only a matter of time before the city fell into our hands. David had spent this entire time in Jerusalem involved in his affairs over Bathsheba and Uriah. By this point in my life, I was aware of the nature of royal politics as well as the fickle nature of human loyalty to a monarch—even one divinely anointed. As I have said before, the army was loyal to me, as their leader. Should Rabbah fall to me, what would have stopped the men from declaring me as their king? I could have rewarded them with the rich spoil. I also knew what a threat I might seem to David's power, should I have conquered Rabbah. In the centuries that followed, only consider how easily the Roman armies were swayed and how easily one emperor after another was toppled. It was no different for us Hebrews, centuries before. I dare say such is the tenuous nature of power even today. And so, I sent a message to my uncle, telling him to bring the remainder of the army and finish off the Ammonites. I even warned him of the danger of what it might mean for him if the city fell to me. I can tell you, Stranger, my uncle had become indolent during my time in the field and had even involved me in his murderous conspiracy. He needed to be seen as a leader in charge. But as you will see, it was perhaps already too late.

For consideration:

- Had you ever considered the trail of death left by David? If not, how did you miss it?

- In this writer's opinion, most people need to learn *how* to read scripture. It begins by simply asking logical questions. Thoughts?

Fourteen

Lust Wins the Day

Or

Like Father, Like Son

A MAN WITH MANY wives, like David, can be expected to have even more children—which, as you can see, is certainly the case. We shall be observing two of them: Tamar and her brother Amnon, the eldest of David's sons. The court journalist tells us that Amnon "loved" his half-sister. Only gaze upon her at this instant, in all her youth and beauty. Now let us look upon Amnon and the way he regards Tamar. What do you see? A look of love or lust? People in your time call this a "spoiler alert." Remember how I told you that the court journalist himself does not render judgment on David? Rather, that judgment comes from God via a third party, the prophet Nathan. Well take note again of the scriptures. It is the court journalist who tells us that Amnon "loved" Tamar, but pay attention to the fact that the court journalist tells us that Amnon makes himself sick over his sister "because she was a virgin, and it was beyond his thinking *to do anything to her.*" Now, my visitor, the court journalist has left us two tantalizing pieces of information: Tamar's virginity and Amon's mental frustration at not being able "to do anything to her." With "virginity" on the table, one need not ponder very long over what that "anything" might be that Amon wishes to do, wouldn't you agree?

But Amnon has a cousin, Jonadab, who is very shrewd—in a scheming sort of way. Listen closely to what he says to Amon.

"Why are you looking so dejected morning after morning, O son of the king? Why don't you tell me?"

Seeking consolation, we hear Amnon's answer: "I love Tamar, the sister of my brother Absalom." (My visitor, note that he doesn't state that she is also his sister by David.)

Jonadab, without further prompting, concocts a plan. "Lie upon your bed and act ill. When your father comes to see you, tell him 'Please have my sister Tamar come to me and give me something to eat, as well as prepare a meal in front of me, that I might eat it from her hand.'"

So Amnon adopts Jonadab's plan and feigns being ill. See him there upon his bed, posing such a pathetic picture. Now enters my uncle to enquire about the health of his heir to the throne. Amnon makes his proposal to David: "Please let my sister Tamar come and prepare some cakes in my presence and feed me by hand."

Is it not a sad pretence? Sadly, the scheme works on the great schemer himself, and David sends for Tamar to carry out Amnon's wishes. Now you will witness the last day of Tamar's happiness in her earthly life. She arrives with the necessary ingredients to prepare some cakes on the brazier in Amnon's room. See the care and attention she pays to her brother, the crown prince. But does she suspect his motives, for when the cakes are ready, see how she empties the pan before Amnon. Continuing his pitiful ruse, Amnon refuses to eat and orders all his servants to leave the room. Hear his childlike plea to Tamar.

"Bring the food into my bedchamber so I might eat from your hand." I ask you, Stranger, what kind of man behaves this way? Yes! You have answered well. A man like his father, David, who lets lust overrule his heart and mind. Now that Tamar approaches Amnon's bed, he seizes her and tells her, "Come, lie with me, my sister!" This is no invitation, but a command—a command to commit incest!

Mark well Tamar's response: "No, my brother! Do not defile me, for such a thing is not done in Israel! Do not do this foolish thing! What about me? Where could I go with my shame? And think of yourself: you would be considered one of the wicked fools of Israel."

Alas, Tamar's words fall on ears deafened by lust. You, Stranger, like me, have no need to observe such violation of this young woman. Yet consider her plea once more, think of her choice of words. For she speaks not simply for herself, but also for the voiceless Bathsheba—not to mention all of her sisters throughout the ages—particularly in a world wherein rape has become weaponized. There is also a bitter irony in her name, in these circumstances, for it means "date palm" or the date fruit itself. And like ripe fruit, is she not being plucked by the immoral Amnon?

Let us now return to this terrible scene. But first, note the words used by the court journalist concerning Amnon. After his unconscionable act, "Amnon despised Tamar with great revulsion; such that his disgust for her was greater than the love with which he had previously loved her." It doesn't take a Solomon to understand that his real disgust is with himself. He has raped his own sister, for God's sake! But his self-hatred is cast onto his aggrieved sibling. Listen to him.

"Get up and get out of here!"

Once more the hapless Tamar begs her brother. "No, my brother; this evil in sending me away is greater than what you have already done to me!"

But calling upon their blood relation has no effect on Amnon. His lust sated and his shame ignited, he remains adamant, and calls to his servant, "Get this woman out of my presence—and bolt the door after her!" Yes, Stranger, the sister whom he professed to love is now only "this woman," so he has Tamar thrown out. As you can see for yourself, Amnon and Tamar are not the only ones who know what has taken place behind closed doors. All of Amnon's servants, who were ordered out before he raped his sister, have no doubt as to what has occurred. This being the case, Tamar tears her garments and puts ashes on her head, crying as she leaves her brother's house. Now note what happens when Tamar goes to her brother, Absalom. Was she seeking solace or revenge? I do not know, for she receives neither. Instead, what you can hear quite clearly is the curious response of Absalom.

"Has your brother, Amnon, been with you?" How does that strike you, my visitor? Yes, of course, Absalom must have been fully aware of Amnon's lustful desire for their sister. But sadly, Absalom's concern for his sister's ordeal is not paramount. "Now, my sister, keep quiet about this, for he is your brother, so, don't take this matter to heart."

I see how you look at me, Stranger. But surely you cannot be ignorant of the fact that even in your life, there are many societies wherein the plight of a woman such as Tamar is not considered a grave concern. Even David, who only learns of Amnon's desecration of his sister sometime after the fact, does nothing to censure his beloved Amnon, heir to his throne. Might you be enraged or amused to learn that Amnon's name means "faithful" or "true" in your tongue? As for Tamar, her earthly journey has become a living death, for she is never to become a wife or mother.

As for Absalom, he both seethes and schemes regarding Amnon. He says nothing one way or another to his brother but nurtures his hatred of Amnon for fully two years. It is at this time that Nathan's prophecy concerning the household of David begins its fulfilment: "The sword shall never depart from your house." See, Absalom is planning festivities for the shearing of the sheep and invites all of the king's sons. He even extends the invitation to his father, but David declines. "No, my son, we will not all go, for we would become a burden to you."

However, it would seem that Amnon has turned down the invitation as well, for hear what Absalom says to his father:

"Will you not let Amnon, my brother, come with us?"

Perhaps David is suspicious—even two years after the rape of Tamar. "Why should he go with you?" Still, as you can observe, Absalom continues to pressure David, who finally caves in and sends Amnon along with all of the king's sons.

Let us now watch Absalom give orders to his servants. "Take note when Amnon is tipsy with wine and, when I say to you, 'Strike Amnon!' then kill him. Don't be afraid. Surely it is I who am commanding you. Be strong and brave!" And so, Absalom's festivity becomes the scene for a grisly murder. David's other sons, not knowing whether they were meant to be the next victims, scatter to the four winds.

Let us now move back to David's palace where you shall discover that false news is not the sole province of your era. Someone, perhaps a servant, I do not know, has managed to reach the palace before any of David's sons. Listen to his dire message.

"Absalom has killed all of the king's sons! No one is left!" David immediately tears his garments and lies prostrate upon the ground. His actions are followed by all who attend him. Now see, my cousin Jonadab makes another appearance. Having advised Amnon on how to snare his sister, Tamar, which began this entire bloody episode, he now comes to allay David's worst fear.

"Do not let my lord surmise that all of the young men, the sons of the king, have been killed, for Amnon alone is dead. For by Absalom's command, this day has been determined since the day Amnon raped his sister. Therefore, let my lord the king not take this matter to heart, fearing that all the king's sons are dead. It is Amnon alone who is dead."

Jonadab's words are soon confirmed, as you can see, for a watchman has caught sight of the king's sons riding toward Jerusalem. In the midst of all this, Absalom has fled to the city of Geshur, where his maternal grandfather is king. And there he will remain for three years. As for David, he is mired in double grief, for not only is his heir to the throne, Amnon, dead, but he has seemingly lost Absalom as well.

For consideration:

- In popular legend, the reign of David is depicted as glorious, whereas in fact it was chaotic, amoral and murderous. How do you think David acquired his Teflon coating?

- For this writer, Tamar's plea to her brother Amnon is among the most poignant words ever recorded concerning the plight of women. Re-read them and see how they impact you.

Fifteen

Return of the Exile

AND NOW, MY VISITOR, you are going to see me in action once more. With the death of Amnon and the self-imposed exile of Absalom, David falls into despondency and inaction. He appears to be in a perpetual state of mourning for his sons. Perhaps they bring to mind the child lost to him and Bathsheba? I don't know. All I knew at the time was that David had let go of the reins of kingship and it was being noticed. David's depression seemed rooted in Absalom's absence. And so I sent to Tekoa—not far from David's homeplace of Bethlehem—for a woman who was known for her wisdom. You may now look upon my conversation with her, as I give her my orders.

"Pretend to be a woman in mourning and dress accordingly. Do not anoint yourself with oil, but act like a woman who has been in mourning for the dead over many days. Go to the king and speak as I shall tell you."

As you shall soon see, she needed very little instruction. Even now she is being admitted into the king's presence. Note what a pathetic figure she cuts falling to the ground before the king and grovelling before him. "Help, O king!"

"What is the matter?"

"I am a widow, for my husband is dead. And your maidservant had two sons who quarrelled one day when they were out in the field. As there was no one to separate them, the one struck the other and killed him. And now all the kinfolks have risen up against your maidservant and are saying, 'Give us the one who killed his brother, so we can kill him for the life of his brother whom he murdered.' They would thereby kill the surviving heir as well, thus extinguishing the ember which remains of my family, thus leaving to my husband neither name nor progeny on the face of the earth."

Now, Stranger, what do you notice about David? Yes, I agree. He has been drawn into the woman's account. Hear how he tells her to return to her house, for he shall give orders concerning her, but note what he adds.

"If anyone says anything to you, bring him to me and he shall never bother you again."

"May the king be mindful of the Lord your God, so that the blood-avenger be prevented from further killing and my son not be slain."

"As the Lord lives, not one hair of your son shall fall to the ground."

———✦———

What is it, Stranger? Your demeanour gives away your mind's inner workings. Shakespeare? Ah, yes, he and his works are often discussed here in life continuing as they lay bare so much of human nature. But no, I am not familiar with Hamlet. Enlighten me.

"The play's the thing wherein I'll catch the conscience of the king." I like that very much! . . . I also wish I had thought of it, but then, I walked the earth as a warrior and not a poet. But you have been an astute observer of David's actions and reactions. Twice now he has rendered judgment on himself by means of a parable or pretense. First by the prophet Nathan and now by the wise woman of Tekoa. She pulled in her king like a hooked fish! My uncle would not seem to have what you today would call "critical insight" as regards his actions. However, the woman of Tekoa is not yet finished with David.

"Please, may your maidservant speak a word to my lord the king? Why is it then, that you have devised such a thing against the people of God? By rendering this decision, the king convicts himself, inasmuch as the king does not return his banished one. All of us must one day die, for we are like water poured on the ground. But God will not deprive of life one who conceives means to return his banished one. Thus, I have come to speak of this to my lord the king because the people have made me afraid, and your maidservant thought 'I will speak to the king. Perhaps the king will accede to the request of his servant. For the king might hear and rescue his servant from the hand of the man sent to destroy me, together with my son from the heritage of God.' And your maidservant thought, 'The word of my lord the king will put me at ease, for my lord the king is like the messenger of God discerning between good and evil.' The Lord your God be with you."

Stranger, have you noticed the shrewd look on David's face? Well then, listen to what he has to say to the wise woman.

"Do not hide from me anything that I might ask you. Do I detect the hand of Joab in all this?"

Yes, my visitor, I am laughing—both at myself and the whole ruse I devised to try to help David resolve his grief over Absalom and return to ruling his kingdom. But let us pause, for the woman of Tekoa is speaking.

"As surely as you live, my lord the king, there is no escaping from all that my lord the king has said. It was indeed your servant Joab who put me up to it and instructed me in all that I was to say. It was in order to change the course of affairs with Absalom that your servant Joab did this. Clearly my lord has wisdom like that of an angel of God to know all matters on the earth."

Now I ask you, my visitor, how was that last statement as a piece of flattery for my uncle? She was a very clever woman indeed. She took a risk in spelling out what her parable meant as regards David, but her obeisance and flattery served her well. And, as you know, David sends for me and asks me to have Absalom returned to Jerusalem. You might as well see me playing the obedient servant of my uncle. See me there, face to the ground, offering my own words of flattery. "Today your servant knows I have found favor in your eyes, my lord the king, for the king has resolved the matter of his servant."

Dear visitor, I did not do this for the sake of my uncle, the king. I did it for the good of the kingdom . . . at least that is what I thought at the time. David made one stipulation as regards Absalom: he could live in his house in Jerusalem, but he was not to come into the king's presence. For me, that seemed like a positive step forward . . . yet if only I had known at the time what the return of Absalom would mean for the kingdom—and for David—but that is as may be and is now all dust. However, let me not get ahead of events. It is time for you to observe young Absalom at work.

First, gaze upon Absalom. He could have posed for Michelangelo's David—if you will pardon the irony! He was known throughout the land as a handsome fellow, from head to toe. The court journalist writes that "there was no blemish." He was even famous for his beautiful, thick hair. Were he alive in your time, he would be a celebrity film star or model! However, as your English adage states, looks can sometimes be deceiving. It is worth noting the court journalist tells us that Absalom had three sons—who are not named. Such is unusual in a patriarchal culture. Yet to Absalom is born one daughter, who is called "Tamar." Think of that, Stranger. After all the years the shame of his sister Tamar is still in his mind. And this daughter is equally beautiful as her aunt.

It is worth taking account of the years. It was two years after the rape of Tamar by Amnon that Absalom killed his brother. Absalom then spends three years in exile. And even after his return to Jerusalem, he is not allowed to see his father for another two years. And this is where I play the pawn again in the complicated relationship between Absalom and David. Absalom sends for me to come to him, but I refuse. Why did I refuse? Frankly I did not approve of the young man. You today would say he had a sense of "entitlement." And as I have already stated, my motive for having him returned was for the good of the kingdom, hoping it would pull David out of his depression. Talk about best laid plans! In any case, Absalom continues to pester me to come to him and I continue to refuse his "summons." Listen to what the scheming little rogue says to his servants.

"See, Joab's field is next to mine, and he has barley there. Go and set fire to it." And that's exactly what his servants do! Look, my barley was nearly ready for the harvest! So, of course I go to Absalom's house to have a word with him.

"Why have your servants burnt my field?"

"Look here, I sent word to you, 'Come here, so that I might send you to the king to enquire: "Why have I come here from Geshur? It would have been better had I remained there."'" So let me see the king in person and if I am found guilty, let him kill me."

And so, Stranger, I did just that and David welcomed his scheming son back into the royal fold. By doing so, my uncle thought he had reconciled his relationship with Absalom. Little was he to know that his troubles were only beginning.

For consideration:

- Are you surprised that appearance sometimes triumphed over substance in biblical times? Keep that in mind as Absalom's story develops.

- Do you find that David's sense of justice seems to be more abstract than existential—i.e., that he is better with parables than with his own actions?

Sixteen

The "Father of Peace" becomes the "Father of Disunity"

It's time to talk of names again, my visitor. This time, it is Absalom. His name means something like "father of peace." It would not stretch the name too far to translate it, "begetter of peace" for isn't begetting what makes a man a father? So hold that in mind as you watch the events that are about to unfold—and very quickly at that! Now that Absalom is back in his father's good graces, he goes about in a chariot with no less than fifty outrunners ahead of him. He behaves as though he were some sort of conquering hero. And he stations himself at one of the city gates—where business is often transacted—intercepting those who have come to see the king for his ruling over some case. Just listen.

"Tell me, sir, from what city do you come? And what business do you wish to bring before my father, the king?" And of course, the man freely tells the king's son his problem or legal case. Now listen carefully for Absalom will—as you say in your tongue—milk it for all it's worth. "Look here, your matters are good and right, but [deep sigh] there is no man appointed by the king to hear you."

See, Stranger, how he portrays himself as a man for the people, compassionate and caring! And now, his *pièce de résistance*! Don't look at me that way, Stranger, for I have had centuries to learn such phrases—as you will learn all too soon, for one's life is always shorter than one realizes. But let's not miss Absalom's next words!

"If only I were appointed judge in the land . . . every man with a lawsuit or case could come to me and I would give him justice."

Ah, the noble Absalom! Usurping the role of his father as judge over the people and acting in the capacity of a quasi-magistrate. Now you can understand why I regret having had him brought back to Jerusalem. And notice how the handsome, empathetic son of the king gives all who pass by him a greeting and a kiss. This goes on for *four years*. And David does nothing to stop it. Yes, my visitor, I too am surprised at how overwrought I am becoming after all these centuries. But then I have rarely revisited past times, for you see, there is more than enough to do to keep up with the world's changes and all the new inhabitants of life continuing. All I wanted was for David to act like the king he was, but instead, he behaved as the man he was. And so, after four years of playing the sympathetic scion of their king, Absalom, as the court journalist tells it, steals the people's hearts. And all of us have to pay the price.

Here is how Absalom frames what he has in mind for his father, David. "Allow me, please, to go to Hebron to pay the vows which I promised to the Lord. For while I was living in Geshur in Aram, I vowed, 'If the Lord will indeed bring me back to Jerusalem, I will worship the Lord.'"

And what does David say to him? "Go in peace."

David doesn't question Absalom as to why Hebron. After all, the ark resides in Jerusalem, so what better place to worship the Lord?

So let us attend Absalom's arrival in Hebron. Even now he is sending out secret messengers to all the tribes of Israel saying, "As soon as you hear the blast of the horn, you shall proclaim, 'Absalom is king in Hebron!'"

So there it is, my visitor. He whose name means "father of peace" has come to Hebron to foment rebellion and civil war. Absalom has bided his time planning this exact moment; thus, he acts quickly and decisively. He sends for Ahitophel—who is one of David's most trusted advisors as well as being Bathsheba's grandfather. Perhaps Ahitophel was a willing accomplice, given the way David took Bathsheba as his own and had her husband killed?

With an insider from David's court such as Ahithophel, the rebellion gains momentum and gathers more followers.

Now we can watch as the penny finally drops for David. Someone is bringing him the news of Absalom's revolt at this moment.

"The loyalty of the men of Israel is with Absalom!"

After allowing Absalom to undermine his authority for four years, David is finally galvanized into action. "Let us get up and flee or there will be no escaping Absalom! Hurry and go, or he will quickly overtake us and bring catastrophe down upon us and destruction to the city."

The court journalist provides a rather interesting detail: David leaves ten of his concubines behind in order to look after the royal house. It seems extraneous to make mention of this, given the dire circumstances in which David finds himself, but it will make sense later. As the now refugee king and his company arrive at the edge of the city, David calls a halt, during which time he has his troops pass in review before him. This could be construed as an odd thing to do in the midst of running for one's life, but, my visitor, note the men-at-arms who accompany David in his flight from Jerusalem. It is something akin to a foreign legion. The court journalist lists them as Cherethites, Pelethites, and "all the six hundred Gittites who had followed him from Gath." It seems they had joined forces with David during his sojourn with the Philistines, when he was on the run from Saul. So here David is again, fleeing for his life, the king of Israel with a bodyguard of Philistines. Certainly, there is more than a little irony in that! It could also be that David simply wanted to see who was left to support him—particularly after being deserted by his chief advisor.

See here how David calls to Ittai, who leads the contingent of Gittites. "Why are you also coming with us? Return and stay with the king, for you are a foreigner and an exile from your home. Why should I make you wander with us to who knows where?"

Stranger, for a king whose own son has turned against him and seeks his life, listen to Ittai's response to David. "As the Lord lives and as my lord the king lives, wherever my lord the king will be—whether in death or in life—there will your servant be also."

"Continue on then."

I see you are surprised by David's terse response. Yes, perhaps he should have shown a little gratitude, but, as you can see, my uncle has been upended by this turn of events. Not to be left behind, the priests Abiathar and Zadok now approach David, along with the Levites, bearing the ark of the covenant. However, David stops them from going further.

"Return the ark of God to the city. If I should find favor in the eyes of the Lord, he will bring me back and let me see both it and its habitation. But if he says, 'I no longer care for you,' then he will do with me as he pleases. See here, go back to the city in peace, you and Abiathar, along with your son Ahima'az and Abiathar's son, Jonathan."

And David, who had danced with complete abandon when the ark was brought to Jerusalem, now leaves it behind, weeping and walking barefoot, with covered head to indicate his state of mourning . . . and perhaps penitence. Look now as a servant approaches David with this message.

"Ahitophel has joined the conspiracy with Absalom."

For my uncle—and the rest of us fleeing Jerusalem—things keep getting worse. All David can do is utter a desperate prayer.

"Please lord, turn the advice of Ahitophel into nonsense!"

Perhaps it was his prayer that God might confound Absalom's plans with foolishness from Ahitophel that gave David his next idea. Hushai the Archite approaches my uncle on the summit of the Mount of Olives. Hushai is one of David's most trusted counsellors and friends, but he is getting on in years. Listen as the king speaks to him.

"If you continue onward with me, you will become a burden. However, if you return to the city, you could say, 'I will be your servant, O king, as I was your father's servant, so now I will serve you.' That way you might confound the counsel of Ahitophel for me. Surely Zadok and Abiathar the priests will be there with you. Thus, whatever you hear from the king's house tell to Zadok and

Abiathar the priests. For their sons Jonathan and Ahima'az are also there and by them you shall send to me everything you hear."

You are right, my visitor, my uncle often had keener wits when he was under pressure. His biggest mistake occurred when he was idle . . . but couldn't we say that about much of humanity? Happily, for David, Hushai agrees to undertake this risky venture and returns to Jerusalem just as Absalom makes his triumphant entry.

For consideration:

- Why do you think David let Absalom undermine his authority over the course of four years?

- Did it occur to you that David's personal bodyguard is made up of a "foreign legion"—similar to when he and his men were the bodyguard of Achish, the Philistine?

Seventeen

An Act of Kindness and Words of Madness(?)

Now, dear visitor, you are about to witness two very diverse encounters between the deposed king and his subjects. Here comes the first. It is Ziba, servant of Meribaʻal, whom you have met before, bringing succor to David and company. His animals are laden with dozens of loaves of bread, bunches of grapes, summer fruits, and wine. David is astounded.

"What are these things of yours?"

"The asses are for the king's household to ride on. The bread and summer fruit are for your servants to eat, and the wine is for anyone to drink who feels faint in the wilderness."

"And where is your master's son?"

Yes, Visitor, why doesn't David thank him? Why ask for the whereabouts of his master's son? Your questions are well put. His "master's son" is Meribaʻal, the son of David's friend Jonathan. And Jonathan, of course, is the son of Saul—David's former nemesis! In one simple question, David has brought up the enmity between him and the house of Saul. David does indeed seem suspicious—but why wouldn't he, given the circumstances?

Now let's hear Ziba's response regarding Meribaʻal's location.

"Well, he remains in Jerusalem because he said, 'Today the house of Israel will return to me the kingdom of my father.'"

Take note of David's immediate response. "See here, everything that belonged to Meribaʻal now belongs to you."

Very generous for a king who no longer reigns, wouldn't you say, Stranger? What else did you notice about David's generosity toward Ziba? Very good! You have learned much of David in your time here. Yes, he accepted Ziba's word without knowing its veracity. What sort of judge makes summary judgments such as that without testimony from the absent accused? Hold on to this question, Stranger, for the court journalist will provide more information before long. In any case, at this moment, Ziba has theoretically become a wealthy man—if David regains his kingship!

And now, my visitor, you are about to see my favorite episode in this sordid affair of Absalom's rebellion. It will unfold presently as we follow David and company a little further eastward. Don't be alarmed. Yes, you can hear his shouting, but you can't see him—yet. It is Shimei, a distant relative of Saul. See how David's past keeps confronting him. Not all of our judgment happens after death. Look! There's Shimei, and he's pelting David and his followers with stones, while saying all sorts of vile things.

"Go away, get out, you bloody murderer! You useless fellow! The Lord has brought upon you all the blood of the house of Saul in whose place you have reigned. Now the Lord has given the kingdom into the hand of your son, Absalom. See, your ruination is upon you, for you are nothing but a bloody murderer!"

I somehow found Shimei's words appropriate—and dare I say, even funny? None of this needed to have happened. Didn't David have enough wives and concubines? How many women does one man need to satisfy his lust? And, yes, I played my part in this ruination of the kingdom. Thus, Shimei's words struck home with me as well. But my brother, Abishai, couldn't stand watching his king being excoriated. Except that David is our uncle, he has less reason to feel offence. Still, he needs to say his piece to David.

"Why should my lord let this dead dog curse him? Let me go over and lop off his head."

"What has my problem to do with you, you sons of Zeruiah? If he is cursing me because the Lord has told him, 'Curse David,' who then shall say, 'Why have you done this?'"

Notice, my visitor, that David has included me with Abishai's impulsive comment: "*sons* of Zeruiah." He often lumped all of us together. But David has not had his final word on the subject of Shimei's cursing him.

"Look, my son who is of my own flesh seeks my life; what then is this Benjaminite? Leave him alone and let him curse, for the Lord has spoken to him. Perhaps the Lord will take note of my iniquity and will return me with good for this cursing of me today?"

And so, my uncle proceeds, with Shimei still dogging his heels, cursing and throwing dirt and rocks at him. David did well not to have Shimei slain. Prophets were often thought to be mad—at least to some degree. They heard voices that the average person could not hear—particularly the voice of God. What might sound complete nonsense to one person could be replete with meaning for another hearer. The import of a message always rests with the hearer.

Discerning Wise Counsel from Deception

Now let us return to Jerusalem to see Absalom's moment of glory as he enters the city. David's former friend and advisor, Ahitophel, enjoys the triumphal entry with him. We also see Hushai the Archite coming into Jerusalem to greet the new king. Listen to the exchange as he greets Absalom.

"Long live the king! Long live the king!"

"This is your loyalty to your friend? Why didn't you stay with your friend?" Absalom is right to question the sincerity of Hushai's greeting and his sense of loyalty. But note Hushai's clever response.

"Not so, my loyalty is with whomever the Lord has chosen—as well as the people and every man of Israel. His I will be, and with him I shall remain. Furthermore, whom should I serve? Should it not be his son? In the same way I served your father, so I will serve you."

Has Hushai actually told a lie? Yes, Stranger, he has deceived, but that is not the same thing as telling a lie. He has stately clearly that he will serve the one the Lord has chosen—and is that not still David? And David was acclaimed king by both Judah and Israel. Neither has Hushai ever named the son he will serve. As for "serving" Absalom in the manner that he served his father . . . well, Hushai is still serving Absalom's father!

Let us now move to listen in on Absalom's war council. He is asking the advice of David's former advisor, Ahitophel.

"Tell us your advice and what we should do."

"Go and enjoy yourself with your father's concubines—the ones he left to look after the palace. When all Israel gets word of this—that you have become loathsome to your father—your cause will be strengthened among your followers."

And so Absalom has a tent set up on the roof of his father's palace and has the concubines sent in to him—for all to see. As Absalom besports himself with the king's concubines, he is at the same time making it clear that he has broken all blood ties with his father and that he is now king.

But Ahitophel has not finished the advice he has for Absalom.

"Let me choose twelve thousand men and I will pursue David this very night. And I will come upon him while he is weary and his strength is spent, thereby startling him and causing all his followers to flee. I will kill only the king, but the rest of the people I will bring back to you and they will be at peace, as you are seeking the life of only one man."

As we can both see, my visitor, Absalom and the elders are pleased by such counsel. Why then does he make his next move, which is to call upon Hushai? Does this traitor to his father not completely trust other traitors? In any case, when Hushai approaches his new king, Absalom tells him of Ahitophel's counsel and asks if he concurs.

"The counsel which Ahitophel has given you this time is not good. You know your father and his men are formidable, and they are incensed like a mother bear robbed of her cubs in the wild. Also, your father is an experienced warrior; he will not encamp with the people. Even now, he is lurking in one of the caves or elsewhere. And when the first attack comes, someone will report, 'There has been a great slaughter among Absalom's followers.' And even he whose heart is brave like the lion's will melt away, for all Israel knows that your father is a fierce warrior and those with him are great fighters. So, my counsel to you is that you gather together all Israel from Dan to Beersheba, as numerous as the sand on the seashore, and that you personally lead the attack. And so we will come upon him—wherever he may be found—and there we shall alight upon him as the dew settles on the earth, and not even one of them shall be left. But, if he withdraws into a city, then all Israel shall take up ropes and we shall pull it down into a wadi until not even one pebble is to be found there."

Well, Stranger, as we can both see, Absalom and all of his conspirators are pleased with Hushai's advice. And while they make their plans, let us follow Hushai as he seeks out the priests, Abiathar and Zadok. He is telling them what he has counselled Absalom and that his counsel has been accepted.

"Therefore, now send quickly and inform David, 'Do not pass the night at the crossing into the wilderness, but make your way over the Jordan before you and all who are with you are swallowed up.'"

So far so good, my visitor, but while the priests' sons, Ahima'az and Jonathan, await the message by a spring on the edge of Jerusalem, the woman who has served as the go-between is spotted by a lad when she approaches them with her urgent message. Meanwhile, the youngster hurries off to tell Absalom. See, even now, Absalom's men are on the hunt for Ahima'az and Jonathan. Along the route which David took to escape the city, they find a friendly woman who lets them hide in her well while Absalom's henchmen search the house. The woman assures the men that the priests' sons have continued on their journey. Once Absalom's men depart, the two messengers climb out of the well and make their way to David, warning of the danger of remaining where they are. David takes heed and he and all his contingent cross over the Jordan before daybreak. Thus, as you can see, my uncle and his men—myself included—head toward the relative safety of Ammonite country.

Perhaps you are not too squeamish to see what happens as regards Ahitophel? You might find it somewhat macabre on my part if I find this short episode amusing, but I have seen it numerous times when I had the need to review my life and actions. There is Ahitophel now, saddling his donkey. It's easy to see he is in ill humor after having his counsel to Absalom rejected. He is even muttering to himself. And off he rides—so let us follow. There! He has reached his destination, which is his home. Instead of seeking to cool his ire with a skin of wine, he goes rummaging in his stable. Look closely at what he has found. Indeed, my visitor, it is a length of rope. No, he is not tethering his donkey with it, but rather, he is about to tether himself! See? He throws the rope over a beam and fastens it tightly. And now he knots the other end around his neck, climbs onto a small stool and kicks it away! Really! Have you ever seen such peevish behavior? Talk about—what do you call it?— "a sore loser?" Ha! What a waste of one's walk upon the earth . . . but then he was a traitor to my uncle and the rest of us. Whatever wisdom he might have shared with David, his end was inglorious stupidity. From this side of eternity, it's hard not to see the humorous side of human self-centeredness and pettiness. What was that, Stranger? No. I have never sought him out here in life continuing. Frankly, I have never had the interest. You see, since I passed over here, there have been far too many others whose lives and experiences have given me much food for thought and contemplation . . . and I think Ahitophel has probably had a great deal to learn himself!

For consideration:

- Considering David's summary executions of messengers who brought him positive news, why do you think he was so patient with Shimei, who cursed him?
- The Messiah was thought of as the one who would restore the "glorious throne of David" . . . what's to restore?

Eighteen

Absalom and Joab Join Battle

I HAVE OFTEN TOLD Sophocles that his Oedipus Rex might have been more interesting had he been able to read Hebrew. For all these events of which you have read and are now witnessing, thanks to your amazing appearance here in life continuing, occurred centuries before Sophocles was born. His florid poetry would have added much to the sparse narrative of the court journalist. In fact, he might have written his tragedy of King Oedipus in a totally different manner. Why look at me with such incredulity? Interestingly, Sophocles agrees with me! Me, the old warrior! This is only a small part of what I meant when I said that there have been too many great souls to meet here than that of poor Ahitophel, though I readily admit he and I are created of the same stuff by the One who has created all. But I digress. Suffice it to say that David and I, along with our army and families, escaped Absalom's pursuing forces and were able to refresh and regroup at Mahana'im—thanks to the help of our former enemies, the Ammonites.

However, our respite is short-lived and soon David seems more of his former self as he resumes his role as warlord. He takes the decision to divide our force into three groups, such that we can fight independently or as one force. I am appointed to lead one group, my brother Abishai, the second and Ittai the Gittite, the third. In some ways, this preparation for the fight with Absalom's army feels like the days when we were on the run from Saul's army. If I say it made me happy, then it was only with regard to seeing David back to his old self and out of his indolent torpor. After forming us into three battle groups, David announces that he is going with us. Perhaps this is out of his paternal concern for Absalom? I don't know, but I, along with many others, immediately insist that David stay in the city. I, for one, was concerned that his father's heart for Absalom might cloud his judgment in battle. In any case, my concerns over David's continuing affection for Absalom are confirmed as we set out for the coming fight. Listen to his final order to Abishai, Ittai, and me.

"Deal gently with the young man, Absalom, for my sake."

Everyone hears him say it. We are about to go into battle to save David's kingdom and yet we are meant to treat his rebellious son with mercy? The son who is at this very moment seeking his father's life? Now you can understand why all of the fighting men wanted David to stay behind. Many of those going out with us will not return home alive this same day—all because of Absalom's treachery. And David asks us to deal gently with his son? Hardly likely!

As it turns out, the battle was fierce but one-sided. Absalom had never commanded troops in battle, so Hushai's ruse to have Absalom lead his army paid off—at least as far as we were concerned. Amid the slaughter and confusion—for we were fighting in a forested area—Absalom encounters some of our men. Look, you can see him now, riding his mule. He heels about, seeking an escape route, only to have his head get caught in the branches of an oak tree. His mule scampers off without him while he is left suspended and helpless. Once more, Stranger, you can sit in the judgment seat regarding my decisions and actions. There I am, receiving a report from one of my soldiers. Let's listen in.

"Listen, I saw Absalom dangling from an oak!"

"What? You saw him? Why didn't you strike him down then and there? I would have given you ten silver shekels and a fine belt."

"Were I to receive a thousand shekels in my hand, I would not raise my hand against the son of the king, for in our hearing the king commanded you, Abishai and Ittai, 'Protect the young man, Absalom, whoever finds him.'"

As you can see, Stranger, I had no time for this delaying. My job was to do what was best for David and the kingdom. And so, when I reply to the messenger, it is curt and to the point. "I'm not going to waste time like this with you!" It was time for action. So, I took three darts and thrusted them into Absalom's chest. And while he was still alive, my armor-bearers joined me and they struck Absalom and killed him. With the rebels' leader dead, I saw no reason for further bloodshed. Thus, I blew the horn and recalled my army from their rout over Absalom's forces. As for the king's disloyal son, we took him into the forest of Ephraim and threw his body into a pit and covered it with a mound of stones. In my opinion, even that paltry grave was more than he deserved.

Zadok's son, Ahima'az, is now approaching me yonder with great excitement. Listen to our exchange. "Let me run and deliver news to the king that the Lord has defended him against the power of his enemies."

"You are not to be the bearer of news today, but you may do so another day. You shall not do so because the king's son is dead." You see, I had an inkling as to how my uncle would respond to such news. I had also seen, as well you know, messengers of questionable news put to death by David. Instead, I gave the task to a Cushite servant, who immediately departed. However, Ahima'az is still not happy with my decision.

"Come what might, please let me run after the Cushite!"

"Why do you want to run, my son, as you'll have no news?"

"Nevertheless, I will run!"

"Go then."

I see that look in your eye again, Stranger. Yes, I allowed Ahima'az to run to David. I thought the Cushite servant, with his head start, would arrive first and deliver the news of the victory over the rebel army and Absalom's death. In any case, you can watch it play out. There, you can see both young men running.

But Ahima'az takes another route, which puts him ahead of the servant, thereby allowing him to reach David first.

Let me ask you, Stranger, have you ever had to give someone terrible news, such as the death of a loved one? If so, then you know that one doesn't simply blurt it out. But neither does one say something inane like, "Remember that son you used to have?" So let us see how young Ahima'az fares in delivering his tidings to David.

"Shalom! Blessed be the Lord your God who has handed over the men who rebelled against my lord the king!"

Yes, that's it, my visitor. He tells the truth—but not the whole truth. I feared as much when I told him not to bring news to the king. Yes, the king has only one outcome in mind: the fate of Absalom.

"How is it with the young man, Absalom?"

"I saw a great commotion when Joab sent the king's servant, that is, your servant, but I don't know what was going on."

Ah, the little weasel. He was all "Send me, send me! I want to tell the king!" And now once he is in the king's presence, he shrinks before the task. Well . . . one can hardly blame him. See, now the Cushite is approaching David, so he has Ahima'az stand aside, as he awaits the second report.

"There is good news for my lord the king! For the Lord has delivered you today from the rebel forces!"

Once again, Stranger, you can see that my uncle's real interest is not in the battle against the traitors in which, I might add, many of our valiant men died. No, his interest lies only within his personal sphere, with his rebellious, patricidal son. And so, the Cushite gives David the news he seeks, but not what he wants to hear.

"May the enemies of my lord the king, and all who rise up against him for evil, be like that young man."

Hearing of Absalom's death, David seeks the privacy of the chamber over the gate and weeps for his dead son. Listen to him.

"O my son, Absalom, my son, my son! O Absalom! If only I could have died instead of you! O Absalom, my son, my son!"

As the court journalist tells us, when the people hear of this, they fall silent and skulk into the city ashamed—like people who have suffered a defeat, rather than a victory—for they do not share David's sentiment for Absalom. They have shared their grief together once, after Absalom's initial rebellion, but that was *then*. *Now*, for the people, David is not a father mourning the death of a son, but a king mourning the death of an *enemy*—an enemy held in common by all the people. He is not acting as a king for the welfare of the nation, rather he acts only to satisfy his own emotions. Although the court journalist seems genuinely sympathetic to David in the way he presents the material, he is also letting us know something about the ultimate weakness and limitation of any human king. As a king, David is now selfish and weak. David, the father, lets the dead Absalom steal the joy of victory from his supporters, just as the living Absalom stole the hearts of all Israel. Therefore, the people are in the same instant both hurt and ashamed, and though victorious for the moment, another division is imminent, if it is not immediately thwarted. When word came to me that David was weeping over Absalom, once again, I knew it was up to me to act. If not I, then who? Once more, my visitor, you may judge my words and actions. There am I now, going to find David in the chamber over the gate. Mark the state of David, bawling his eyes out.

"O my son, Absalom! O Absalom, my son, my son!"

"Today you have brought shame upon all the faces of all your servants who have saved your life and the lives of your sons and daughters, as well as your wives and concubines, for you love those who despise you and despise those who love you. For today you have made it clear that commanders and servants are as nothing to you. For well I know today that if Absalom were alive and all of us had died, then that would have seemed fitting in your eyes. Now get up and go out and speak thoughtfully to your servants, for I swear by the Lord that if you do not go out, no one will remain on your side tonight and it will be worse for you than all the evil that has befallen you from your youth until now."

Yes, Stranger, I took a real and substantial risk in speaking to David that way, inasmuch as he was my elder, my uncle and my king. But I needed to address his indolence and thoughtlessness, particularly with regard to those who had just helped save him and his throne. And this I did, but at a cost to myself, as you shall see.

So, David heeds my warning, ceases his mourning over Absalom and leaves the chamber. He takes his place in the city gate where the people may see him and come before him, and from whence he can oversee his victorious army returning from their defeat over the rebels. All seems to be in order.

For consideration:

- Ah, royal families . . . as I write these words, the House of Windsor is ripping itself apart with revelations of jealousy, enmity and more. Is there indeed anything new under the sun?

- Are there times when a monarch or national leader must actually rise above human emotions? Is it possible?

Nineteen

It Ain't Over until It's Over

As you have no doubt discovered in your sojourn upon the earth, my visitor, life is rarely straightforward. There are always unexpected twists and turns, and so it is with David's return to power. With your permission, I shall take you on a quick return to the aftermath of the battle between David's and Absalom's armies. This will involve a tour among the various tribes of Israel as they squabble over the reinstatement of David as their king. We see David by the River Jordan waiting, as it were, to hear the tribes' declarations of loyalty to him as their king. The northern tribes or "Israel"—as opposed to the southern tribes, referred to as "Judah"—assert that, although many of them chose to anoint and follow Absalom, they have now reasserted their allegiance to David. Judah is David's home territory, yet they react more slowly to the news of David's return to the throne. You can hear frustration in his own words in the message he sends to the priests, Abiathar and Zadok.

"Say to the elders of Judah the following: 'Why are you the last to bring the king back to his house, when the word of all Israel has reached the king in his household? You are my kith and kin, so why are you lagging behind in returning the king?' Also say to Amasa, 'Are you not a kinsman of mine? May God do to me and more so if I do not make you commander of the army in place of Joab!'"

Why am I laughing? It's because of the look on your face, my visitor! I thought you might have remembered from the scriptures David's removing me from leadership of his army. Some thanks indeed for saving his position as king by galvanizing him into action. Of course, I find it funny now. First, it is so far in the past—despite our watching it play out again. Second, I had killed one of the king's sons—to save David, it is true—but he never forgave me for this action, and it only led him to heap more malice on me along with my having killed Abner. Both of these actions were to preserve his position as God's anointed, but David always seemed incognizant of that fact. I could have left him to fight it out with Abner and the army of Israel and I could have left him at the mercy of Absalom, but loyalty to David was a fickle business. And you haven't seen the worst yet! Wait until I die! We'll get to that in due course. But here we are, with Amasa being made commander over the army. Amasa, the very one who led Absalom's army of rebels! The irony really is too rich, don't you agree? Go ahead! You too can laugh. I am long beyond the time when such things could injure my pride.

Interestingly, it is with his appointment of Amasa as leader of the army that the holdouts from Judah finally pledge their allegiance to David as their king—for the second time! Next, we can watch the procession of former rebels as well as those of questionable allegiance come and profess their loyalty to David—even Shimei, who had pursued David and his followers out of Jerusalem, cursing them and pelting them with stones! It really is too funny! So many people—both Jews and Christians—look back to the time of King David as Israel's glory days, when in fact all of our hands were covered in the blood of our relatives! Oh certainly, people such as the English do the same with the reign of Elizabeth the First, but even then, consider how many of her courtiers had a way of losing their heads! So many monuments are erected to "our glorious dead," but as you are witnessing here in life continuing, the dead might not always agree that their deaths were glorious. Rather, they might have cherished more days upon the earth to walk in the warmth of the sun with their loved ones.

And so the professions of loyalty quickly become a shouting match. Israel professes its numerical superiority over Judah, and Judah claims its kinship with the king! Each camp has the need to be right or be given preferential treatment. Now you are laughing with me. That's good! Human nature hasn't changed in the nearly three thousand years that have separated our times upon the earth, has it? Adults are no better behaved than children squabbling over a toy; they are simply better at pretending they know what they are doing!

During the ensuing chaos, a man named Sheba, a Benjaminite, whom the court journalist describes as "worthless," blows the horn and calls out: "We have no interest in David, and we have no inheritance in this son of Jesse. Every man to his tents, O Israel!"

By sending everyone to "his tents," my visitor, he is effectively telling them to desert David and follow him. And you are right, Stranger! It's *déjà vu*! Yet another civil war. But the court journalist also provides us with a fascinating morsel of information. Immediately after Sheba's declaration of independence from David, we are told that David went into his royal residence and removed the ten concubines whom he had left to care for the house and "put them in a guard house, and had them cared for, but he never again had relations with them, so they were closed away until the day they died, living as widows."

I ask you, Stranger, how bizarre is that? If you had just learned of yet another revolt, would your first concern be concubines who had been used by your rebel son? No doubt someone had informed David, but once more, his injured pride takes precedence over his acting like a king. I, of course, was in disfavor, so there was no one to speak plainly to my uncle. Thus, the king turns to Amasa, and orders him to rally the army to David within three days, and to be there himself. But what does Amasa do? He dawdles. Perhaps he still wishes that Absalom had become king? Who knows? But in his absence, David calls upon my brother, Abishai. Look now.

"Now Sheba, the son of Bichri, will do us more harm than Absalom! Take your lord's servants and get after him, lest he finds fortified cities to occupy and escape us."

Observe there, my visitor, as my brother takes charge of the Philistine contingents, as well as David's best fighting men, and goes in pursuit of Sheba and his army. Note that I am there among them. I believe that David couldn't face the fact that he had made a grave error in judgment when he appointed Amasa in my place, so instead of calling me, he summoned my brother—whilst not forbidding me from going along with the army. As we come to Gibeon, just northwest of Jerusalem, whom do we meet but Amasa—that lazy turncoat! Once more I put you in the judgment seat regarding my actions. Note that as I lay hold of his beard—apparently to kiss him—he doesn't notice the sword in my left hand. That omission is soon remedied as it finds a home in his belly. Yes, it is probably well that you turn your head, for he is laid open with one blow. One of my men makes Amasa's body our "line in the sand." Listen to him.

"Whoever favors Joab and whoever follows David, let him follow Joab."

And with that, my visitor, I am back in command of David's army, once again saving his reign, but you will never hear David speak a word of gratitude—only the opposite. Except for those with a bloodlust—and there are and have been too many of them—they rarely count the cost in human lives that it takes to keep them in power.

And so, the fighting men once more flock behind me as we go in pursuit of Sheba, who has fled to the northernmost reaches of Israel, to Abel-Beth-Ma'acah, near Dan. There it is. See? And what else do you see, my visitor? That's right! Once more I am preparing for a siege. As I have said before, it is such tedious work. Do you think I liked it? Notice that my officers and I are searching out the most vulnerable part of the city's defenses. Once we have made the assessment, our men set to building a siege ramp. Others are hewing a large tree, suitable for work as a battering ram. And once more, it is our own kinsmen we are preparing to kill. But such was the reign of my uncle, David.

Now witness something curious indeed. There on the wall. Another one of Israel's wise women. Listen to her shout above the din of battle.

"Listen! Listen! Tell Joab, 'Draw near for I want to speak to you.'"

I can tell you, Stranger, there were those among my men who thought this might be a trap to kill me, but as before, I found myself having confidence in this wise woman. And so, you can witness our conversation.

"Are you Joab?"

"I am."

"Listen to the words of your maidservant."

"I'm listening."

"In bygone days, people used to say, 'Let them go seek advice in Abel,' and thus was a matter resolved. I am one of the peace-loving and faithful of Israel. You are seeking to destroy a city which is a mother in Israel. Why will you devour the heritage of the Lord?"

"It is certainly not my intention to swallow up or destroy. That is not the case, for there is a man from the hill country of Ephraim, called Sheba, the son of Bichri, who has rebelled against King David. Give him up alone and I will depart from the city."

"See here, his head shall be thrown over the wall to you!"

Notice how she reasons with the people that by putting to death the outlaw, Sheba, the rest of the city might be saved. And with that, they relieve Sheba of his head . . . he hadn't used it very advantageously anyway, had he, Stranger? And so, I blew the horn and my men and I set off for Jerusalem. All of us were glad not to have to sit out another siege! And so ended the second revolt of David's kingship. For my part in quelling the rebellion—and in the absence of Amasa—I retained my position as head of David's army.

Aftermath of Sheba's Revolt:
One Famine . . . and Seven Hangings

As if David and Israel had not been through enough trying times, drought and famine follow the revolt of Sheba and his clan. The country suffers for three years before my uncle is given a message from the Lord. Well, at least he claimed it was from the Lord. Why do I say that, Stranger? Quite simply because David was seeking relief from the famine, whereas the message given to him is . . . well . . . hear it for yourself from David's lips.

"As for Saul and his house, there is bloodguilt, because of his killing the Gibeonites."

Frankly, Stranger, I know of no such incident. Was it, perhaps, Saul's killing the priests in *Gibeah* in the days when he sought David's life? Has the compiler of the court journalist's records erred? Again, I do not know. That remains between David and the Lord. What I do know is that David asked the Gibeonites what they would have him do. But note what the court journalist writes: "Let seven men of his offspring be given to us that we might hang them at Gibeah of Saul, God's chosen."

Yes, you do well to be puzzled, Stranger! And you are not alone. Many have tried to scrutinize the meaning of the "divine" message received by David and the grim request of the Gibeonites. Ah, dear visitor, I can see the question in your eyes! Is it what *do* I think *now* or what *did* I think *then*? Let's just say there are those who have mused that having survived two rebellions against his rule, receiving "divine" instruction to wipe out more of Saul's heirs as a means to quell the famine could be construed as a convenient method to eliminate any other contenders for the throne. I am not saying this is a fact. It is merely one way of making sense of the confusion. But there is more. Do you not find it curious that the Gibeonites—in David's presence—refer to Saul as "the Lord's chosen"? Does this not add weight to the idea that Saul's offspring are a continuing threat to the security of David's reign? The court journalist has written what David has asked him to record.

In the event, David hands over seven men of Saul's lineage to be executed: two sons and five grandsons. Yet David takes measures to protect Meriba'al, the son of David's best friend and Saul's son, Jonathan, and he would have been in direct line of succession to Saul's throne. As ruthless as my uncle could be, he also had a doggedly loyal and, perhaps even sentimental, side . . . I think he was quintessentially human, with a combination of what is both best and worst in humanity.

There is one thing I think you should see. We are now in the wake of the executions, and Rizpah, Saul's concubine and mother of his two remaining two sons—now deceased—comes to where the bodies have been left in disgrace, unburied. Rizpah brings the sackcloth of mourning and spreads it out as a ground-cloth, and there she keeps company with her dead sons, shooing away the birds of carrion and wild beasts. Let me ask you something, dear visitor. Are you familiar with the play, *Antigone*, by Sophocles? As you know, I have spoken with him here, in life continuing. We discussed the similarity of his play and the actions of Rizpah. In sum, Antigone and her two brothers were the children of Oedipus, king of Thebes. After their father's death, the two brothers were meant to share the kingdom, by ruling in alternate years. However, the older brother, who ruled first, refused to relinquish the throne, so the two brothers quarrelled and fought a duel—in which both of them died. The queen's brother, Creon, became the king and decreed that the younger brother's body would not receive proper burial rites as he had rebelled against his city. Here is the point: Antigone would not marry her lover or even rest until her brother had been buried. She could not live her privileged life as long as her dead brother lay in the open as food for wild creatures. For her loyalty to her brother, she paid with her life. The Greeks liked their tragedies; we Hebrews lived them!

As a father who has lost several of his sons, when David learns of Rizpah's selfless dedication to her sons' remains, he takes her pitiful situation to heart. Certainly, David's dearest friend, Jonathan, as well as his father, had suffered a similar fate after their deaths in the battle of Mount Gilboa. Their bodies had been hung on the walls of the Philistine city of Beth She'an, until spirited away by brave Israelites. Thus, David orders that the bones of Saul and Jonathan, along with the bones of the seven hanged men, be collected and buried in the land of Benjamin, in the tomb of Saul's father, Kish. But note what the court journalist tells us: "Following this, God was moved by the prayers for the land." And what were the prayers for the land, except for an end to the famine? Shall I leave you to puzzle over that for a few moments, my visitor? Then you can tell me what you think. Why not re-read the passage again or shall we revisit the actions?

⟿

Good. You are ready to reveal your thoughts or questions? Yes, I see. There is indeed a contradiction between the purported reason for the famine—the bloodguilt of Saul and the need for human sacrifice (itself forbidden in Israelite tradition!)—and God's heeding the supplications for the land. On the one hand, does the Almighty actually require blood sacrifice in order to provide rain? This is contradictory to the scriptural tradition. On the other hand, the way the court journalist puts it, it was David's providing a proper burial place for Saul, Jonathan and their slain kin that satisfies the Lord. And yes, it can add credence to the argument that David killed Saul's offspring in order to prevent yet another rebellion. And it was his honoring these same dead that brought about the rainfall to end the famine! Alas, whether we blame the court journalist or the later scribal editors for the confusion, it seems we are very often left with mystery in the scriptural record. You have learned much in your time here!

For consideration:

- Isn't it fascinating how often these accounts in Samuel have turned on the advice of a wise woman? It is also the case that in both Hebrew and Greek, the word for "wisdom" is feminine.

- Although Israel was a patriarchal society, is it not intriguing that these countercultural accounts of wise women have survived? Or perhaps in our modern arrogance we have made assumptions about the past which are not accurate?

Twenty

A Bizarre Interlude

THERE IS NOT A lot else to say or see as regards David. There were intermittent battles with the Philistines, to be sure. Although David went out with the army, he found he could not withstand the physical demands of battle. My brother, Abishai, had to rescue David from one of the Philistine champions, after which our men insisted that David no longer go into battle with the army of Israel. And so, my uncle remained in Jerusalem, where he wrote his poems and psalms of praise and thanksgiving to the Lord . . . in any case he was no longer philandering! At least you are laughing, Stranger! In your world, people talk about "taking the long view." Well, you, because of your curiosity—and perhaps brazenness in coming here to life continuing—have had the experience of the long view . . . very long indeed. As a result, the rest of your earthly walk will never be the same. You will find that problems that once seemed of supreme importance will have now shrunk to a mere bother, and things that once seemed of such immense value will have lost their lustre. But you will laugh more and—dare I say— love more? That is my main regret from my time on the earth: I did not simply enjoy *being alive*. My life was subservient to my uncle, who was at the same time my king. I protected his throne, fought his wars at the expense of not having enjoyed a family, love, and laughter. All life is recycled cosmic dust. But this is not to say it is without meaning—just don't be one of those who leaves it until life continuing to discover the real joy of human existence.

Before we witness David's end—and mine—there is one more curious incident I think you should see. It is the court journalist's last entry in the Samuel scrolls. The court journalist writes that, "Yet again the anger of the Lord was stirred up against Israel and he incited David against them, saying, 'Go and number Israel and Judah.'" My uncle calls upon me and says he has received a message from God to conduct a census in response to God's anger. Bizarre, isn't it? And so, David gives me the following order:

"Go about all the tribes of Israel from Dan to Beer-Sheba and take a count of the people, that I may know their number."

Is this not an odd thing for a military man to do? And so, I question my king. "Would that the Lord your God might add to the people a hundred times more than they are, and that my lord the king might see it, but why does the lord my king desire such a thing?" As you can hear, Stranger, my response to David's order is met with skepticism. To this day, I wonder about some of the "oracles" my uncle received. Nevertheless, as a soldier, an order is an order, so my men and I went all about the kingdom, numbering the people of every tribal area. I don't mind saying this exercise took us nine months! Not exactly the best use of Israel's army. I felt that then and even today.

Pardon my excursus, for we will return to the action, but . . . what I have learned *here* and what I *now* know to be the case, is that the Lord allows for a measure of randomness in our lives. Or, as some wit of your time has said, "Shit happens." The book of Job—which was not available to me in my time—makes randomness in human life patently clear. The only answer to the "why" of unfortunate circumstances is our individual attitude. That's it. We can scream and cry and thrash ourselves about or we can recognize that we will never know all of the facts surrounding a situation. We only have control over our responses and choices. It's so easy to fall into the mistaken notion that we are the masters of our own fate—and even the fates of others, especially if we have some measure of power. But this is only self-delusion. We are all of us absorbed in something much greater than the individual human enterprise.

So then, I report back to David the number of people in the kingdom—let's not quibble about figures. But what response do I receive after nine months' work? Just listen to David as he pours out his heart to the Lord!

"I have sinned gravely in what I have done, so please, Lord, take away the iniquity of your servant, for I have behaved foolishly!"

Go ahead, my visitor—ask the questions that I can feel bursting from your spirit. Yes, of course! Haven't we only just heard from David that it was the Lord who commanded him to carry out a national census? So why indeed is he claiming the responsibility? Was it perhaps an act of hubris on his part? It could well have been. But once more I have to tell you that I don't know. I can assure you that you will have more puzzlement when you witness what happens next.

God sends word to David through David's prophet, Gad, saying, "Three fates I hold over you; choose for yourself one of them, that I may bring it upon you. Shall three years of famine come into your land? Or shall you flee before your enemies while they pursue you for three months? Or shall there be three days of pestilence in the land? Think it over and see what it is I shall tell the One who sent me."

"I'm too befuddled! Let us fall into the hand of God, for he is full of compassion . . . but don't let me fall into the hand of man!"

What's that, my visitor? Yes, David has contradicted himself by saying in essence "let God sort it out," but then he dismisses the second fate: being pursued (again!) by his enemies.

So, is God angry with David or Israel . . . or both? And is God punishing David, Israel . . . or both? The court journalist has told us *exactly nothing* about why God might be angry with the people, and it is David who claims the responsibility for God's displeasure, yet it is the people who pay the price for his guilt! Yes indeed! Shit does happen! And more is on the way, as we can now witness. Having ruled out being hounded by his enemies—my uncle had certainly had enough of that!—it is left to God to choose between three years of famine or three days of pestilence. And who gets to suffer—the people!

I suppose God was being lenient when the decision was made for three days of pestilence. My visitor, I suggest only a brief look at the results. It was uncharitable of me, but at the time I felt aggrieved that so much of my and the army's time had been wasted counting people, many of whom would wind up dead shortly thereafter! But as I said earlier, all life is but recycled cosmic dust.

For consideration:

- What purpose could a census have served—for David or God?

- David could have placed the punishment for the census upon himself: three months of flight from his enemies. Instead, he left the decision to God to choose which punishment should befall the *people of Israel*. What kind of leader does that?

Twenty-one

Endings and Beginnings

WHILE THE SAMUEL SCROLLS make mention of David's final words, we must turn to the Kings' scrolls for the account of David's death and mine. I hadn't actually given it much thought until your visit, my visitor, but I suppose having lived a life that stretched over three scrolls is no small matter in human terms! That Joab's name should be spoken after nearly three thousand years to some degree overrides my ignominious end. But of that you shall be witness soon enough. First to my uncle.

There he lies under a pile of bedclothes—and even still he is cold. Gone is the hot-blooded warrior, adulterer, murderer, poet, king, musician. Now he is like a fire which has been reduced to grey, smouldering ashes. Listen to his servants.

"Let a young woman, a virgin, be sought for my lord the king, let her wait upon the king and be his carer, and let her lie in your bosom, that my lord the king might be warm." And as the court journalist tells us, David's servants sought for a beautiful young virgin throughout the territory of Israel. Their choice was Abishag the Shunnamite from the vicinity of Mount Gilboa. Her beauty was unquestionable, and she became David's nursemaid and bed partner, but as the court journalist tells us, "The king knew her not." Yes, the journalist/scribe uses the puritanical turn of phrase which was used regarding Adam and Eve. In other words, my uncle did not have sexual relations with her. So, my randy old uncle really was on the way out!

Meanwhile, Adonijah, David's oldest surviving son, has taken his father's impotence and dotage as a signal for him to claim the throne for himself. According to the court journalist, he was a very handsome lad—like his older brother, Absalom—and had been spoiled by his father. I thought Adonijah's was a reasonable position. After all, it was the way of most monarchies: the eldest assumes the throne. Thus, when he approached me and Abiathar, the priest, we naturally gave him our support. Adonijah then goes to offer sacrifices to the Lord in confirmation of his kingship. He does not invite Zadok, Nathan or Benaiah, who commanded David's "mighty men" nor does he invite Solomon. Perhaps he was already aware their loyalties lay elsewhere.

However, Zadok, the other priest, and Nathan, the prophet, did not support Adonijah. Hence, much in the same way that David's anointment to kingship began, so it ends: with a rift in the kingdom. Nathan, whose wisdom and judgment I had never heretofore doubted, becomes the schemer. Mind you, I only fully learned of this after I came here! Listen to his conniving with Bathsheba, the mother of Solomon.

"Have you not heard that Adonijah, the son of Haggith, has assumed the throne, and our lord, David, is not aware? Now, therefore, let me offer you a piece of advice that your life might be saved, as well as the life of your son, Solomon. Go at once to King David and say to him, 'Didn't my lord the king swear to your maidservant that Solomon, your son, would rule after me and he shall sit upon my throne? Why then is Adonijah king?' So, while you are still speaking with the king, I shall enter and verify your words."

What's that, my visitor? Yes, it is ironic that Nathan, who had so roundly condemned David's affair with Bathsheba, is now taking her part! But there's more. Only observe.

See, there is Bathsheba, going to David and speaking the words given to her by Nathan. She elaborates by telling him of the sacrifices offered by Adonijah. "He has sacrificed oxen, and fatted cattle, and sheep aplenty. He has also invited all the sons of the king, Abiathar the priest, and Joab the commander of the army. But Solomon, your servant, he has not invited. Now, as for you, my lord the king, the eyes of all Israel are upon you to tell them who will sit on the throne of my lord the king after him. Thus when my lord the king sleeps with his fathers, I will be—along with my son, Solomon—criminals."

Bathsheba is followed by Nathan, who spins the same story, but adding that the sons of the king, Abiathar and the commanders of the army "are eating and drinking in front of Adonijah, and proclaiming, 'Long live king Adonijah!' But as for me, your servant, Zadok the priest, and Benaiah the son of Jehoiada, and your servant Solomon, he has not invited. Has this thing been done by my lord the king and yet you have not told your servant who should sit on the throne of my lord the king after him?"

Why am I laughing, you ask me? Haven't you been listening, my dear visitor, to all of the grovelling—"my lord the king this and my lord the king that"? Such conniving! What was that you said? Repeat those terms please, for I am not familiar. "Elder abuse"? "False memory?" Let me see if I understand you. In your time and place, to treat an elderly person, such as my uncle, in such a way as to convince him of things he has never said or done, would be considered implanting a false memory? And it would constitute abusive behavior toward a vulnerable older person. Hmmm . . . I like that. Perhaps some things have indeed changed for the better.

But alas, in the event, we hear David succumbing to the verbal onslaught from both Nathan and Bathsheba. "Call Bathsheba to me!" Now see how innocently she appears before her dying husband.

"As the Lord lives, who has redeemed my life from every hardship; as I swore to you by the Lord God of Israel, 'Indeed, Solomon, your son, shall be king after me and he shall sit upon my throne in my place' and I shall surely do this today." Bathsheba bows so obsequiously and humbly before her husband the king.

"May my lord King David live forever!"

Ha! You are quite right, dear visitor. She is probably thinking, "May my lord King David die as quickly as possible," to secure her son as king and ensure her position as the queen mother. What puzzles me about people of the Judeo-Christian faith is how few of them even notice this cruel and deadly trick that is played on my senile uncle, the great King David. Can they not read for themselves? The court journalist has never written *anything* in his account about David's naming Solomon as his heir to the throne and swearing an oath to that effect to Bathsheba. To quote a man wiser than I: "You may fool people for a time; you can fool a part of the people all the time; but you can't fool all the people all the time." Too many people of faith are indeed fooled all of the time— but by themselves! All that which you are witnessing here in life continuing—is it not written in the scriptures? So where do people come up with such idealized notions about my uncle—of his son, Solomon?

Nevertheless, let us see David as he plays the king for the last time, acting upon the ruse planted in his mind by a dishonest prophet and a grasping wife. Although, to be fair to Bathsheba— with three thousand years hindsight!—perhaps this is her vengeance on David for raping her all those years before . . . and for the loss of her first child? On this occasion, Bathsheba has David in her hands like a plaything. But let's hear him speak.

"Call to me Zadok the priest, Nathan the prophet, and Benaiah, the son of Jehoiada."

One of many things I like about life continuing is that no sooner does David speak than the three men appear before him— none of the waiting about as in earthly time!

"Take with you the servants of your lord and have my son, Solomon, ride my personal mule, and take him down to Gihon. There let Zadok the priest and Nathan the prophet anoint him king over Israel. Then blow the horn and proclaim, 'Long live King Solomon!'"

This action of my uncle's is, of course, my death sentence. So let us observe the ensuing chaos brought on by a meddling prophet and a power-hungry wife of David. You can see their entourage heading down into the Kidron valley: Zadok, Nathan, Benaiah, along with David's personal guard, and Solomon. It's a very short distance from the royal palace. Immediately they arrive at the Gihon spring, Zadok takes the horn of oil and anoints Solomon. Someone blows the horn, and all the people shout, "Long live King Solomon!"

Now let us turn our attention to the parallel celebration of Adonijah's kingship. Note my perplexity at hearing the tumult of Solomon's entourage. "What is this din coming from the city?" As though in answer to my question, now enters Jonathan, the son of Abiathar the priest, as I am still speaking. Adonijah believes he is bringing good news, but he is sadly mistaken.

"No! For our lord King David has made Solomon king, and he has sent with him Zadok the priest, Nathan the prophet, and Benaiah the son of Jehoiada, as well as the Cherethites, and the Pelethites; and they have mounted Solomon on the king's mule. In addition, Zadok the priest and Nathan the prophet have anointed him king at Gihon, and they have ascended from there to the city which is in an uproar. This is the commotion you are hearing. Solomon sits on the royal throne! And in addition, the servants of the king have gone to bless our lord King David, saying, 'May your God make the name of Solomon even better than yours and make his throne even greater than your throne!' And the king responded, 'Blessed be the Lord God of Israel, who has today placed someone to sit on the throne, and I am able to see it.'"

And with that, dear visitor, you can see that panic breaks out among the host of Adonijah's supporters, with no one wanting to stand by him, but rather putting as much distance between him and themselves as possible. Seeing his precarious situation and fearing what Solomon might do, we now follow Adonijah to the tent of the Lord where he seizes the horns of the altar. Why, you ask? It's like the word "sanctuary" used in your culture today, itself stemming from a medieval notion that one could escape punishment by seeking sanctuary in a church or holy place. He hopes not to be slain by his younger brother. Hear then the message he sends to Solomon: "Let King Solomon swear to me today that he will not put his servant to death with the sword."

And now we turn our attention to the palace, where we can hear the young king's response to his brother. "If he proves himself to be an honorable man, not one of his hairs shall fall to the ground; but should deceit be found in him, he shall die."

Upon receiving this message from Solomon's servants, we see Adonijah leave the altar and go to the royal palace, where his younger brother simply says the following: "Go to your house." Yes, I can understand how you have heard this short speech from Solomon to his older brother as patronizing. Indeed, it is like being told, "Go to your room." Of that, we shall see more momentarily; but let us see David's end.

For consideration:

- For this writer and Hebrew scholar, I confess that the machinations of Nathan and Bathsheba lay hidden in plain sight for years. It is only as I carefully re-read Samuel (numerous times!) that I finally recognized the trick pulled on David. But then, hadn't Nathan prophesied that because of David's murdering Uriah and raping Bathsheba, the sword would never depart his house? Once more, it is an innocent man who must die: Adonijah.

Twenty-two

Promises Made and Broken

LOOK, THERE HE LIES on his bed, with the young Solomon seated nearby—the son he has been duped into declaring king. Let us hear his final earthly words.

"I am going the way of all the earth. So be strong and show yourself to be a man, and keep the charge of the Lord your God, by walking in his ways and obeying his statutes, his commandments and his ordinances and his testimonies, as it is written in the law of Moses, that you might prosper in all that you do and in any direction you turn; that the Lord might prove his word which he spoke concerning me: 'If your sons keep their way, to walk before me in truth, with all of their heart and all of their soul, you shall not be without a descendant upon the throne of Israel.' In addition, you know what Joab the son of Zeruiah did to me, what he did to the two commanders of the army of Israel, Abner the son of Ner, and Amasa the son of Jether, whom he killed and shed the blood of war in peacetime on the belt which was around his waist and on the sandals on his feet. Do according to your wisdom, but do not let his grey hair go down to Sheol in peace! But to the children of Barzillai the Gileadite, act with loving loyalty and let them be among those who eat at your table, for so they greeted me when I was on the run from Absalom, your brother. And there is also with you Shimei, the son of Gera, the Benjaminite from Bahurim, who cruelly cursed me when I went to Mahana'im, for he came down to the Jordan to meet me. Yet I swore to him by the Lord that 'I will not put you to death by the sword.' But *now* do not let him go unpunished! For you are a wise man and know what to do to him that you might send his grey hair down in blood to Sheol."

And these, dear visitor—according to the court journalist or perhaps his successor—are my uncle David's last words. They are words of vengeance upon both those who challenged his right to be king, as well as those, like myself, who supported—and even saved—his kingship. That blood-vengeance should be a man's last living thoughts is indeed a sad commentary . . . but at least it was consistent with my uncle's life—even though he was also condemning me, his own nephew, to death.

Truly, I see you are bursting to say something, so please go ahead. Yes, Shimei, poor soul. Indeed, you are right again: so much for David's oath in the Lord's name! It is not his first, but it certainly is his last lie. Taking the Lord's name in vain? But of course. I suppose that after his having broken many of the Ten Commandments—coveting his neighbor's wife, adultery, murder, theft—perhaps he thought taking the Lord's name in vain could not make matters any worse. And besides, he was dying. One could also blame it on his dementia or simply see it as integral to my uncle's life of grasping for power. I have never asked him.

Sadly, he now includes Solomon in his bloodlust. Isn't it once more ironic—if not comical—that although David tells Solomon, "You are a wise man and know what to do to him . . ." he finishes the sentence by leaving no doubt that he wants Shimei dead(!), for he adds, ". . . that you might send his grey hair down in blood to Sheol." Thus, Solomon's first charge as king is to carry out the death sentence for his father's perceived enemies. Yes, it seems the sins of the fathers are indeed visited upon the children.

There remain only a few scenes left in this tragedy, if you will. So let us return to Adonijah. See now he approaches Bathsheba, the mother of Solomon. Bathsheba seems somewhat taken aback by his presence, don't you think? Listen.

"Do you come in peace?"

"Yes, in peace. I have something to say to you."

"Speak."

"You know that the kingdom was mine and that it was on me the people set their expectations to become king. The kingdom has changed hands and is now my brother's, for it was his from the Lord. Now I have one request to ask of you—don't turn me away."

"Speak."

"Please speak to Solomon the king—he will not refuse you— that he might give to me Abishag the Shunammite for a wife."

"Very well, I will speak to the king on your behalf." And off she goes to her son, the new king. Now this is funny—well, it wasn't at the time, but again, after a few thousand years . . . *well*. Oh, but I'm about to spoil the fun for you. Look there, young Solomon rises and bows to his mother. Now we see who is the real power behind the throne!

"I have one small request to ask of you; do not refuse me."

"Ask, my mother, for I will not refuse you."

"Let Abishag the Shunammite be given as a wife to your brother, Adonijah."

Look how enraged this upstart king is becoming!

"And why is it you ask Abishag the Shunammite for Adonijah?! Ask for him to have the kingdom as well, for he is my older brother! On his side are Abiathar the priest and Joab the son of Zeruiah. May God do so to me and more indeed if his broaching this matter doesn't cost Adonijah his life! Therefore, as the Lord lives who has established me and set me upon the throne of my father, David, and who has made a house for me, just as he promised, Adonijah shall be put to death today!"

And so, Solomon sends Benaiah the son of Jehoiada to kill Adonijah. There! Now please tell me what you think of this sorry business. Yes, it is hard to know where to begin, is it not?

Ah, yes! Once more we have promises made and broken. Solomon says he won't deny the request of the very woman—his mother—who put him on the throne, and then immediately breaks his word. At least you're laughing now, dear visitor. It is another case of like father, like son. And then all of the swearing by the Lord, who Solomon says placed him on the throne. Utter rubbish.

I totally agree. It was that rascal, Nathan, and David's scheming wife, Bathsheba, who engineered Solomon's accession to the throne. He might have well claimed it was fate. Perhaps Adonijah overstepped the mark by requesting for a wife the latest addition to his father's harem, Abishag the Shunnamite. After all, the harem is part of the new king's inheritance; but one gets the notion that sooner or later Solomon would have found a way to eliminate his older brother—his promises be damned.

As for Abiathar the priest, as a holy man he is shown clemency, for he had loyally served with David and suffered along with David when there was civil war in the country. Solomon expels him from his priestly duties and banishes him from Jerusalem to live on his property in Anathoth.

So now there is one: I, myself, me—Joab—David's loyal servant and your host here in life continuing. It doesn't take long for the news of Adonijah's assassination and Abiathar's banishment to reach my ears. So, like Adonijah, I too flee to the tent of the Lord and lay hold of the horns of the altar. I freely admit to you, dear visitor, that in my time on earth, I was not yet ready to die—if I could avoid it. I thought "Why should I, who have served my king so faithfully, die at the hands of his upstart son, who has never tasted battle and spilled other men's blood, that he might inherit all that I helped his father establish?" And so Benaiah, who now plays the role of Joab for Solomon, comes to the holy tent to carry out his blood-soaked orders. Let us not draw this out, for well you know that I had to die in order to be where you now find me! So, there I wait in the tent of the Lord—and now enters Benaiah.

"The king says, 'Come out!'"

"No, for I will die here."

As you can see, Benaiah reports back to his king my refusal to leave. He quickly returns with the order to kill me where I stand, and so he strikes me dead—in Israel's holiest place. Well, as I said before, I was never a spiritual man in earthly life . . . and now, that's all I am! So in the end, I suppose he did me a favor! And you have to agree the irony in my death is delicious! Oh, Solomon's court recorder writes that I was killed for the crime of shedding "righteous blood," and quotes Solomon as saying that the blood of Abner and Amasa "will return on the head of Joab and on the head of his descendants forever . . . but as for David and his descendants and upon his house, and his throne, *there shall be peace forever* from the Lord." This, of course, conveniently overlooks the Lord's curse upon the house of David that was pronounced by the prophet Nathan, following David's affair with Solomon's mother! "The sword *will never depart from your house*, because you have scorned me and have taken the wife of Uriah the Hittite as your own." The crowning irony is that Nathan himself willingly becomes a fulfillment of the prophecy he delivered as he aids and abets the death of Adonijah, David's son, and myself, David's nephew—both of us being of David's household.

Was I justly killed or unjustly murdered? This I leave to you, dear visitor. You have now witnessed all these events for yourself, so I shall let you be the judge of my life and actions. Such things are no longer important to me. But, in Solomon's cursing me and blessing his father's house with "peace forever"—well again, I must laugh at the irony of it all! And I am heartened that you can join me! No, of course, my uncle's reign was anything but peaceful! And as for eternal peace over the house and throne of David, the kingdom was ripped asunder after Solomon's death and has remained so until your time on earth.

Before you depart—for depart you must—may I ask what you have come to understand better about David? Ha! Dear visitor, you have a way of making this spirit laugh! "The problem with kings is their princes! Only witness Amnon, Absalom, and Solomon." Well-stated! Yes, they, like their father David, are quintessentially human. And, yes! Legends are what we create to sanitize our past, our shared history. In earthly life, we all like to think we descend from greatness of one sort or another. But here in life continuing we learn that greatness consists in what both surrounds and upholds us all. And until we meet again—for I trust we shall—be mindful that all life has echoes, and that you are in the process of becoming forever what you freely choose and love most in life. Live well. Shalom.

For consideration:

- Was Joab ever disloyal to David? Did he deserve to die for defending the very throne inherited by Solomon?

- In the popular imagination of both Jews and Christians, there is much positive imagery attached to the house of David. However, once one has discovered that his house and reign were founded on murder, intrigue, rebellion, warfare and more, for this author, the restoration of the house of David loses its attraction. And you?

- How has this book impacted your reading of scripture?